*Tell You All*

Contact the publisher

agerton9800@hotmail.com

# Tell You All

*E. David Brown*

Plateau Press
Montréal, Canada

Printed in Canada
Printed by Transcontinental Printing, Montréal, Canada
Cover illustration by Arik Brauer

To Terry Ades, my wife, lover and most demanding critic;
Flannery Brown, my daughter and critic in waiting (learn
from your mother); Sue Stewart, my dearest friend and
sounding board; T.F. Rigelhof, who took time off from his
own novel to read my work and offer me advice; and Arik
Brauer, who gave me permission to use his haunting work
*Autumn* as the cover illustration of the novel.

Plateau Press, Montréal, Canada

Canadian Cataloguing in Publication Data

Brown, E. David, 1951-
    Tell you all

ISBN 0-9684117-0-3

    1. Lazarus (Biblical figure) — Fiction. I. Title.

PS8553.R684954T45 1998     C813'.54     C98-901195-X
PR9199.3.B6976T45 1998

I am Lazarus, come from the dead,
Come back to tell you all, I shall tell you all

- T. S. Eliot,
*The Love Song of J. Alfred Prufrock*

# 1

Flies swarmed above the plain, casting a single shadow across the dung and refuse heap on the outskirts of Bethany. Moses had fulfilled his quest, brought his people out of bondage to be enslaved by a vision of milk and honey in a land that barely provided bread and water. As fresh waste was tossed on the heap, the flies circling above landed as one body and deposited their eggs on the muck. Famine, drought, and never-ending wars were the legacy of the inhabitants of this land.

The crowd gathering outside the clay house since dawn made its presence known. A rock crashed against the hovel's door. Inside the house, Mary glared at Martha and Rachel as they cowered in the corner.

"Get up. We must be prepared to greet Him."

Standing off by herself, Sarah avoided contact with the three sisters. The old woman rubbed one ancient hand over the other to soothe the pain in her swollen knuckles.

The din of angry villagers intensified. "Idiots," Mary snarled. She smoothed back her cropped hair and scrunched her nose at the fetid stench of meat gone bad.

Mary and Martha made a point of visiting their little sister at least three times a year to recount the latest miracles the man from Galilee had worked. They had returned again, ostensibly to comfort Rachel and her mother-in-law, Sarah, in this difficult time.

Their own mother had accompanied them on this visit. The one thing Deborah had in common with Sarah was her displeasure at her daughters' devotion to the mystic whom she called "an ignorant nail-pusher" when she referred to him at all.

"Rachel, light some incense," Mary ordered as her eyes fell on the body laid out on a rough board suspended between two saw horses.

"I said light the incense."

Another rock slammed against the door. Mary hiked up her cotton pantaloons and cinched the belt tighter around her thick waist. She whisked away the flies circling the body.

The muscular frame, extending over the length of the six-foot plank, was sculpted by two decades of hard labour. Three days after his demise the corpse had started to succumb to the indignity of decay and putrefaction that all animals, even those created in Hashem's image, must undergo. Well-defined biceps and powerful thighs, gained through years of hauling slabs of stone and wielding hammers and chisels, were beginning to lose their solidity.

A man from outside shouted, "Give him to us."

Sarah shook a walnut-coloured fist at Mary. "He's right. What you're doing stands against our laws."

Mary sniffed the air again. "We need more sandalwood."

"He was your husband," Sarah pleaded with Rachel.

"It's not important what he was," Mary said. "The only thing that matters is what he will become."

Martha, who spoke rarely, and only then in cryptic phrases, smiled. "We're waiting for His coming."

"Yes, for His coming," Rachel mumbled.

"It won't be long," Mary said. "I sent word for Him to come."

Sarah unbolted the door and flung it open. "My boy is not part of your delirium."

The first person through the entrance was Jacob, the burly owner of the local grind-stone. He gasped when he saw the remains of his friend on the table, naked except for a cloth over his genitals.

"Cover him!" He stood to the side to allow three members of the village burial society to enter. They looked at the corpse and retreated from the room. An uninterred corpse was an anathema. The malevolent spirits of Gehenna which lurked behind the shadows of the living were known to enter the dead.

Sarah snatched the winding sheet from their hands and stumbled toward the body of her son. She tried to tuck the sheet beneath the corpse. Shamed by the sight of the old woman struggling to lift her son, Jacob slipped his hands under the cadaver's back, held his breath and raised it to a sitting position. Sarah quickly finished her task. Jacob released the body. The liquid inside the corpse shifted. It landed on the plank with a pulpy thud. The trapped gases escaped, filling the room with a noxious odour.

Four migrant beggars who had been pressed into service on their way through the village were shoved into the room by the crowd. The vagrants reluctantly lifted the plank and carried the body through the doors.

Mary grabbed a stick from the fire pit, ploughed her way through the crowd and ran in front of the litter carriers. "Rachel, Martha! Get out here!" Her sisters timidly manoeuvred their way around the people and stood by Mary's side.

"Wait! The one whose coming was foretold is on the way to work a great miracle."

Jacob strode toward Mary. "Get out of the way."

Mary planted her weight on the flat of her soles. She lunged, jabbing the stick into Jacob's stomach. Before she could thrust the stick again Jacob's knuckles connected with her jaw. Mary fell into the arms of her sisters.

Jacob clamped his huge hand around her jaw. "Do you know the law, our law?" He pushed her head back and peered into her glazed eyes.

"Don't harm her." The villagers parted to make a corridor for Sarah. She clutched the wrist of a tall, straight-backed woman, an older, more severe version of the sisters. The woman glared at Mary.

Sarah nudged her to the front of the crowd. "Let their own mother deal with them."

The woman's face was frozen in a scowl. She approached the three sisters and stretched out her arm. "Whore!" she screeched.

Mary turned her cheek. Her mother drew back her hand and slapped her. "Is it not enough that you have disgraced yourself; must you drag your sisters into your shame?"

Mary turned her other cheek to receive another slap. "Go back home, Mother. There will be no Shibah, no mourning for you to feed on here."

Deborah spit in her daughter's face.

The spittle trickled down Mary's cheek. She spread her arms over her sisters. "They're believers. They know He'll come to judge the quick and the dead, restoring the chosen few to life, free of the corruption of the grave."

Rachel fluttered her hand at the corpse and sang, "Emmanuel will reveal His love through my husband."

"The Shabbat is approaching. It's too far to make it back to your village before sunset. Leave on Sunday and take your daughters with you." Jacob turned away from Deborah to Sarah. "I warned your boy about marrying outside our village. No good ever came from mixing seed."

The burial procession walked for over an hour before arriving at the bottom of the camel-humped row of hills. Jacob sought out a path leading to the caves at the crest of the rockiest incline. He scaled the hill and halted in front of the yawning mouth of a grotto that lay apart from the other sealed caves peppering the face of the hills. On reaching the top the litter bearers lowered their burden. Sarah, accompanied by the three sisters, threaded her way through the group of men.

"Don't stay here. Go away!" Jacob choked out the words.

Sarah's body trembled. "He's my son. I have the right to see that Kaddish is said for him."

"There will be no Kaddish." Jacob's voice trailed off when Eli, the village baker, handed him a cudgel.

Eli's fat tongue poked in and out of his hog face. "To say a prayer for this thing will bring down the wrath of God on all of us."

"No Kaddish." A wall of men formed between Jacob and the women. "Evil resides within this body. We must release it to free the soul." He raised the cudgel above his head and brought it down on the face of the corpse.

Sarah fell to her knees and crawled between the legs of the men. She threw herself over the body and pulled back the shroud. Her son's features were mashed beyond recognition. The blow had flattened the nose across his face, obliterated the eye socket. The eye dangled like a rotten grape on the pulverised cheekbone.

The cudgel slipped from Jacob's grasp. "I warned you to leave."

Sarah folded her legs under her and rent the front of her robe. "*Yitgaddal ve-yitkadadsh —*" A fleshy hand pressed itself over her mouth.

"You heard him," Eli said. "No Kaddish. "

"There's no need to weep." Mary stood on her toes and shouted at Sarah above the heads of the men. "On the judgement day, those who believe will return from the dead and live in the promised kingdom as they were in life."

"You've done enough, said enough." Jacob's arm swept the ground to retrieve the club. He pounded the air. "Three days. You have three days to leave."

The litter bearers hastily covered the corpse and carried it inside the cave. They dumped the body on the ground and rushed out to search for rocks large enough to seal off the tomb from the rest of world.

# 2

Sarah appeared in front of one the dried mud houses that stood out against the beige backdrop of hills rising above the desert. Cooler than the flatlands, the hills were pocked with caves which once provided sanctuary for David from the king he loved.

She crossed the village square to the communal well, perfectly erect, refusing to be hunched by her eighty years. Two clay pots were suspended from the yoke she carried. The yoke was notched in the middle to fit over her neck. Its weight was spread equally and braced against her shoulder blades. Sarah glanced up at the hills. Twelve of her children rested in its caves. Denied the right to say Kaddish, she resolved to do what she did best, survive.

Sarah bowed her head as three Roman soldiers walked by. To look into the faces of the soldiers was to challenge their authority. They had arrived on Shabbat with a scouting party of Bedouins to scour the countryside for Zealots. Ever since the radicals had launched their campaign to reclaim the land, garrisons of the clean-shaven idolaters had sprung up throughout the country. Their mission: preserve the Pax Romana.

Caesar tolerated no insolence from his subjects. Trees decorated with the rotting corpses of outlaws and rebels ensured the Roman peace was respected. When the soldiers were out of sight, Sarah sucked in her cheeks and spit in their direction. The wind rose without warning, creating a dwarf cyclone of dust in front of her. She gagged on a curse and pulled the dirty rag encircling her neck over her mouth and nose.

Sarah groaned as she lifted the yoke from her neck and placed it on the ground. She was the first person at the well today. The other women were still inside their homes. Sarah could draw her water without being subjected to their taunts and malicious gossip. In a land lacking everything but promises, it was the small victories that counted.

The well's crumbling walls were even older than Sarah. Its teak-coloured waters had quenched the thirst of her people before they were a people, before her ancestors had abandoned their nomadic wanderings to scratch out an existence in the land Moses had led them to. She picked up a bucket the villagers used to draw water, wrapped both her hands around its rope and lowered it into the well.

"Looks like you need help."

Startled by the sound of a man's voice coming from behind her, Sarah nearly fell into the water. A sinewy arm shot out and pulled her away from the well's edge.

She howled, "First you see fit to drown me and then you save me?"

Her rescuer was dressed in white, another one of the wandering mystics who had abandoned Qumran, a retreat from the temptations of the secular world perched on a butte overlooking the Dead Sea. These itinerant ascetics travelled throughout the countryside offering redemption to those who took an oath of simplicity, piety, truthfulness, and justice. When all of Abraham's people heeded their message the Anointed One would appear.

"It would be better for all of us if they would stick to their prayer cells and let the Messiah find them," Sarah muttered.

On her son's single journey outside the village to purchase some tools, he had brought back a wife. Though incapable of baking bread, Rachel was able to recite verbatim the drivel she had heard a new pretender to the title of the "Chosen One" relate to the masses. Her sisters were even worse than she was, confirmation to Sarah that lunacy ran in the girl's family. If he had asked, Sarah could have told him Rachel was deranged and perhaps the grotesque spectacle that had been acted out three days earlier on the slopes near Bethany would have been avoided.

The stranger took the rope from Sarah and pulled up the bucket from the bottom of the well. Water sloshed over his forearm when he poured its contents into the clay pots.

"I don't need your help."

"Consider it a mitzvah." His long red hair tumbled over his forehead. He reached up and brushed it out of his eyes. His fingernails were ragged, his hands large, callused. He secured the jugs to the yoke and placed it behind his neck.

"That's my water." Sarah stood on her tiptoes and tried to take the yoke from him.

He stepped around her and started toward the village.

Sarah scooped up a fistful of sand and threw it at him. "What do you want from me?"

"Want?" He looked directly into the sun. "Does Hashem ask for anything but your love when he gives you life?"

"How should I know? All I've received from Him is an incessant case of dyspepsia and flatulence."

"Perhaps that's all we can ask for until we change our ways." He stopped to survey the village. "In a town of this size, I imagine you must know everyone."

Sarah scanned the distant hills before answering. "It's harder to keep track of the dead here than the living."

"Then you must know a stonecutter by the name of Lazarus."

Sarah coiled her fingers into a fist, digging her nails into her leathery palms. "They buried my son three days ago."

The mystic's nostrils flared. He breathed like a bull. "What do you mean you buried him?"

Sarah responded in a monotone that cloaked her anguish, "Not me. His friends." The last word lingered in her mouth like the taste of curdled milk. "His friends took care of him."

"That complicates things." The mystic's benign smile invited Sarah to place her faith in him. "Shouldn't you be at home sitting Shibah for him?"

"Someone has to fetch the water." Sarah wanted to tell him that every day she awoke, her life was dedicated to grieving for her children.

"Take me to his home."

"Unless you're Elijah there's nothing you can do for him."

"Elijah was only a prophet."

Sarah smacked her lips over her toothless gums. She nodded at a house standing on its own at the end of the village. "You carry the water."

It was not easy for Sarah to keep up with the man. He barely left a footprint in the sand. He took long, seemingly weightless strides.

"Who better than a mother to confirm a miracle?"

Sarah looked around to see whom the stranger was addressing. No one was there, except for a few nosy women on their way to the well.

"Of course, you're right." The man cocked his head to the side as if listening to someone whispering in his ear. "I'll need her and the others as witnesses."

Sarah reconsidered her invitation. The land was full of bandits. What if the man's real motive for gaining entrance to her home was to kill the inhabitants, before making off with what few possessions they owned? Screaming for help would be futile. Chances were the villagers would stay inside their homes. Over the last three days they had become immune to her tirades.

Sarah raced to catch up with her water. She heard the prattling of women from inside the hovel. The man pushed open the door and entered without knocking.

Mary, Martha, and Deborah sat around the crude table. On the floor was Rachel, her eyes fixed on the hard-packed dirt. She stood up to greet the man when he stepped into the dim light provided by the open doorway. The only other source of illumination came from two holes hacked out of the front walls.

15

Sarah sniffed the air. The scent of burnt bread and sour wine mingled with the musky aroma of the desert brush used to fuel the cooking fire.

The stranger extended his arm. Rachel fell to her knees and allowed him to place his hand on her head.

"I've been on the road for for a week. I'm tired and hungry." Before anyone could respond he repeated, "I said I'm hungry." Deborah pushed the chair away from the table and started to say something but instead clamped her mouth shut and stalked out of the house.

"Your mother never did think much of me, did she?"

"She's not a believer." Mary placed her hand over a charm in the shape of a fish dangling from a chain around her neck. She reached out to touch his cheek and brought her fingertips back to her lips. "Martha was afraid you wouldn't come."

The stranger frowned. "The days are approaching when all will wish they had placed their faith in me."

Mary pulled a wash basin from under the table.

"No, not you; I know you love me. I am here for her." He levelled his eyes at Rachel.

The young widow scurried on all fours to the man. "Master, sit down." Rachel lifted his feet and placed them in the basin. "Mother Sarah, bring me water."

"He almost pushes me into the well, takes my property without my permission, invades my house without so much as introducing himself, and you expect me to wait on him?"

"He has come a long way for us."

"If he's come this far, then it won't kill him to walk over here and get his own water."

"He is a guest in this house."

Sarah turned her back on her daughter-in-law. "Your guest, not mine."

Carefully enunciating each word, Mary said. "When my sister's husband died, this house became hers."

"Then let her get the water."

Mary brushed past the old woman and brought a water jug over to her sister. Sarah recoiled when Rachel poured the vessel's precious contents over the man's feet.

The stranger placed his hands behind his neck. He leaned back, using the cup formed by his locked fingers as a cradle to support his head. "I've come to help."

Rachel pulled her skirt above her knees and bent over the basin.

"You're six days too late." Mary stood behind him, kneading his shoulders between her fingers. "He's dead."

"I know." The mystic felt obliged to vindicate himself. "It's not my fault. I had a wedding to do. It lasted longer than I expected. By the time it ended the party was so drunk it couldn't tell water from wine."

"Well, you're here now."

"I couldn't pass up the opportunity. Although I admit I would have preferred to arrive when he was somewhat more ambulatory."

Mary worked her thumbs into the back of his neck. "Are you afraid we lack faith?"

"No, I'm just disappointed that there will be no one except us to witness my work here today," he sighed. "It would have been better if you could have kept him longer. That way, at least, I'd have something resembling a crowd to inspire me. I always perform best when there's an audience."

Rachel glanced up from the man's feet. "He was bleeding from the nose, coughing terribly. It was a blessing he died when he did."

"That's not for you to decide." The stranger lifted one foot out of the basin.

Sarah kept her rancour in her heart as she watched her daughter-in-law wait on the stranger.

Rachel removed the scarf covering her head. "We put him in a cave in the hills above the village." She shook loose her long hair and used it to dry his feet. "We have been waiting for you to bless him."

"What business does he have saying blessings for my son? Benedictions are for the living!" Sarah screeched.

"Take me to his grave."

Rachel tied her hair back with the kerchief. She placed his foot on her lap and rubbed oil into the sole of his foot and the back of his heel.

"What good would it do to visit a grave that even I, his own mother, have been warned is cursed?"

Rachel coyly tilted her head and rested her cheek on her shoulder like a child waiting for approval. "First have something to eat and drink, then I'll take you there."

"You have no business running up and down the hills. This is the time you, we, should be sitting Shibah for my son. Even if it means doing it in secret."

"Only those who hear the good news and deny it should be mourned. Those who die and yet believe in me shall have everlasting life." The stranger raised his eyebrows at the old woman. "That is the gospel."

Sarah's head wobbled when she replied, "No, that's blasphemy."

"If it is, then it's between my father and me."

Rachel walked to the fire pit. She came back with a wooden bowl filled to the top with fava beans. Her guest devoured the beans and sopped up the brown liquid at the bottom of the bowl with a piece of flat bread. She poured wine into a wooden goblet. He drained the cup and wiped his mouth across the white sleeve of his robe. Rising slowly from his seat, he belched.

"We have to hurry. I have rendezvous with Peter in Capernaum to plan for my arrival in Jerusalem." He marched to the door. The sun cast his shadow into the hovel. "Take me to Lazarus. "

Rachel and her sisters joined the stranger. Sarah remained in the house. The man crooked his finger at the old woman. "Come on, don't hold back. There's a reward in it for those who follow me."

"I don't want any part of this. Leave me alone." Sarah attempted to shut the door but was prevented from doing so by Mary.

"Follow us. The Master has promised you a reward for coming with Him, something that will mean more to you than a fading memory of your son."

A tremor of anger passed through Sarah's entire body. She considered lambasting Mary with whatever invectives she could think of, but remembered it was rumoured that these travelling mystics carried silver with them. Surely her son wouldn't begrudge her the chance to afford a measure of oil for his memorial lamp. Sarah waited until the mystic and the women had established a good lead before starting after them.

Three men crossed the square and blocked their way. Eli had one arm behind his back. He snorted and pawed the earth with his foot. "I thought we told you to be out of here by today."

Mary charged the baker, knocking him off balance. "Actually only Martha and I were told to leave. Sarah and Rachel belong here."

"See this?" The baker whipped his arm out from behind his back. He shoved a large stone under Mary's nose. "When the sun reaches midday, if you and your sisters are still here you'll learn how we treat apostates."

The stranger stepped forward. "Stop wasting my time, little man! My mission on Earth is coming to a close."

Eli dashed over to the mystic and juggled the rock in front of him. "I don't know who you are. But I warn you, if you are a friend of these bitches, you'll get the same medicine as them."

The stranger stretched his arms to the heavens. He looked into the sun and exclaimed, "Yes, Father, Your will will be done." Without a hint of warning his elbow came down on the dome of Eli's head. The baker crumpled to his knees. He looked up in mute pain while his two friends ran off. The mystic kicked the rock that had fallen from Eli's grip across the square. "Let he who is without sin cast the first stone."

The three sisters responded with a chorus of "Amens," parading single file behind the mystic and out of the village.

Sarah lagged behind the group. She snickered when she walked past Eli. "Serves you right. Maybe he drove some decency into that knob you call a head."

The parched earth gave way to marginally greener scrub growth the closer they came to the hills that offered an escape from the

19

flatlands' insufferable heat. Sarah pulled off the rag covering her face to allow the breeze to cool her.

Rachel ran ahead of the group. She crouched at the bottom of a hill and looked up at a mound of rocks piled at the entrance of one of the caves. "They put him in that one."

Of all of Sarah's children, Lazarus was the only one who did not share a cave with his siblings. Sarah bit her lip. She tried to force herself to bring forth tears. It was no use. She had no tears left.

The mystic scrambled up the slope, causing a small avalanche of pebbles to gather at the feet of the women. He immediately went to work, unpiling the heap of rocks and sheets of slate sealing off the tomb.

Sarah tried to climb the hill. "Leave my boy's grave alone," she cried out and picked up a piece of wood. She was unaware that the weapon she wielded was the same cudgel used on her son's corpse.

The stranger took no heed of the old woman's protest and continued his task. After a few minutes he sat down on a boulder. He wiped away the sweat trickling down his forehead into his eyes. "Help me!"

Mary drove Rachel and Martha up the hill past Sarah. "And we will beat swords into ploughshares," she said and jerked the club out of Sarah's hand.

Sarah looked on in disbelief as the women scurried up the hill and took up where the stranger had left off. The sisters worked together to lift the largest of the rocks and roll them down the hill. In a few minutes the opening was large enough for a person to squeeze through. The stench of decaying flesh seeped out of the hole they had created.

Sarah rushed toward the opening of the cave and started piling rocks in front of it. "That's enough. Have you no respect for the dead?"

The stranger thrust out his lower jaw. "Don't interfere."

Martha and Mary grabbed the old woman.

"Rachel, stop this madness, if not for me then for the sake of your husband," Sarah implored.

The young woman covered her ears and sang, "For His is the power and the glory forever and ever."

The man smiled at Rachel. "She's right, you know." He leaned over to peer into the darkness of the tomb, pulled his head back and gulped down fresh air.

Sarah tried to break out of the grasp of the two women. "Did you think it was going to smell like lilacs?"

"Be still. He's concentrating," Mary said.

The stranger wiped his palms on the front of his robe. "I've never done anything like this before."

When the two women relaxed their grip, Sarah broke free and raced over to the stranger. She placed her bony hand on his shoulder and looked into his face. Her visage was frozen in the irises of his green eyes, eyes that glowed but held no warmth.

Mary dragged Sarah away from the mystic. "Stay put. The Master has a difficult enough calling without having to worry about you."

"Well here it goes." The stranger flung his arms over his head. "Lazarus, I command you to arise!"

Nothing happened. The voice of the stranger echoed throughout the dark cavity of the tomb. Sarah moved her index finger in a circle next to her temple. Rachel and Martha chanted softly as they stared at the ground.

"Lazarus, get up." The corpse inside the tomb remained a corpse.

Mary steered her sisters over to the mystic. The women squeezed one anothers' hands.

"Okay now," he cued them, "Lazarus, arise!"

"Lazarus, arise!" the sisters chanted at the top of their lungs. In unison they dropped to their knees. Again nothing happened. The stranger sat down on his boulder, staring dejectedly at the tomb.

Mary massaged his rope-like neck muscles. "Maybe he isn't the right one," she consoled him.

"You selfish bastard," he cursed and jumped up, shaking a fist at the cave. "Come on, Lazarus, is it so much to ask? Think of your wife and mother. They hiked all the way here just to see you."

The unbearable stench of putrid flesh permeated the cave. Lazarus opened his eyes and stared into the darkness. The last thing he remembered was gagging on the soup his mother had forced down his throat when he was confined to bed with what he believed was a cold. In stages, his limbs regained sensation and mobility. Enveloped in his winding sheet, he rose from the slab of moist stone. Placing one foot awkwardly in front of the other, Lazarus groped his way through the black tomb. He slumped to his hands and knees, crawled toward a shaft of light piercing the darkness at the front of the cave. He felt a waft of fresh air.

Lazarus groaned as he shoved away a large stone lodged at the mouth of the tomb. A huge grey slug, he slithered out of the cave on his belly, entering the world of the living a second time, head first. He rose from the warm earth like an enormous protuberance of fungus growing from the body of some great beast. Like slivers of glass being forced under his eyelids, the sun's rays tortured him. His blackened fingertips fumbled with a loose piece of cloth dangling from the side of his head. He unwound the shroud. As he did so, his hand sunk to its knuckles in the hollow left by the blow of the cudgel. He had no memory of the event.

"My son!" Sarah's voice climbed to the peak of joy only to lapse into silence when the cloth covering Lazarus' face fell away.

The stranger danced around the motionless stonecutter. "I did it. I did it." Martha and Rachel fell prostrate before the mystic. Their incoherent prayers were mingled with sobs and exclamations of terror.

Like a child learning to take its first step, Lazarus lurched toward his wife. He stretched out his arms in front of him, opening and closing his fists as if waiting for someone to awaken him from this nightmare. He buried his chin in his neck and gazed at Rachel. She pulled her legs up to her chest, blanketing her head with her arms.

Rachel screamed when Lazarus took a faltering step and brushed against her. The ruptured surface of his skin was teeming with vermin. Up until now the bugs had feasted on the exterior of the cadaver. Given a few more days, they would have burrowed their way to the delicate organs inside the husk. Lazarus moved his mouth trying to formulate words but only succeeded in articulating a low moan.

"Damn you." Sarah's curse sought out the stranger.

"Show some gratitude," Mary said. "Remember, you are his mother."

"That is the one thing I will never deny." Sarah stroked the side of the face that still bore a resemblance to her son's. The mould growing on Lazarus' cold flesh came loose under her fingertips.

"He stinks." Mary circled Lazarus. "You said that those who trust in you will be resurrected uncorrupted on the day of judgement."

"I did. They will. But that day has not arrived yet. And besides, this man's revival is the product of your faith, not his. He does not know me."

Mary clicked her tongue over her teeth. "Maybe once we get him cleaned up he won't look so bad. "

"Leave that to his mother and his wife." The stranger pressed his lips to the back of her hand. "I need you and Martha to help me prepare for my journey to Jerusalem."

"Who will take care of them?" Mary rolled her eyes at Rachel, who was desperately trying to disappear into her robe.

"That's not our concern. I have accomplished what I came for. Now it's time for us to spread the word of the marvel you have witnessed."

Lazarus stared at the old woman's face. A spark of recognition flickered in the one eye remaining to him, the other having turned into a feeding trough for maggots. Sarah pulled her hand into the cuff of her robe and used her sleeve to wipe away the putrid mess seeping from his dead eye socket. She opened her arms. Lazarus stumbled into her embrace.

Mary called out, "Rachel, see what joy our Master has wrought."

Rachel curled herself into a ball. Gibberish punctuated with shrieks of praise for the stranger spilled out of her mouth. Martha tried to lift her but failed. Rachel kicked at Martha when she persisted in her attempt to make her stand.

"This is your miracle, horror and madness?"

The stranger dismissed Sarah's query. He started down the hill. Sarah seized the back of his robe. "Return my son to me like he was before or send him back to the grave. What you've given him is neither life nor death."

The stranger yanked himself free of Sarah's grasp. "When he regains his senses let him know that there is a meaning to all this. Just as I was sent here to serve my Father's purpose, Lazarus was resurrected to serve that same purpose." The stranger paused and cleared his throat before bellowing like a peddler hawking his wares in front of the Temple in Jerusalem. "If anyone asks who worked this miracle, tell them it was Jeshua of Nazareth. If they ask who this Jeshua is, tell them I am the Alpha and the Omega."

The old woman pushed Lazarus out in front of her. "Tell him why you have brought him back."

"To prove that the deliverer of our people whose coming was foretold by Elijah has arrived." Jeshua's moist lips turned red as he warmed to the topic. He spouted the standard platitudes that over the centuries had become part of the routine of all the Messiahs who had appeared since the conquest of the kingdoms by the Babylonians. When Jeshua finished he strode down the hill and onto a path leading away from the village. Martha and Mary followed him.

"Wait!" Sarah shouted.

"Oh yes, I forgot about your reward." His hand flitted above his head. He spoke without looking back, "For those who believe and follow me the kingdom of heaven is their reward."

Sarah guided Lazarus by his forearm to where Rachel lay shivering on the ground. "Wha…" Lazarus made an unfathomable noise. He placed Sarah's hand on his mouth. She felt his lips crack. He tried to move his tongue but it remained fixed to the bottom of his mouth. She held her breath when he exhaled the mephitis of the tomb. He gurgled at first, struggling to speak.

"Wha…" He put his palms on both sides of Sarah's head and held her steady. His self-loathing on seeing his mangled countenance trapped in Sarah's eyes was magnified when he looked at his young wife.

Rachel, resting on her side, her knees cocked to her throat, chanted tunelessly, "His kingdom come. His will be done. His kingdom come. His will be done."

Sarah knelt beside Rachel, stroking her hair until she was quiet.

"What for!" A terrible voice, hollow and distant, escaped from Lazarus. "Come back!" His words were swallowed by the hills.

## 3

Young boys, some of whose chins barely came up to the ledge of the rock wall, stood on sentry to catch a glimpse of the creature who wandered through the pillars of granite and marble inside the stonecutter's work yard.

The grown-ups had cautioned them of the danger of standing too close to the wall, filling their heads with tales of the beast's insatiable appetite for children. When the boys retreated, the adults cast curses and the occasional handful of dung over the wall at the abomination that dwelt in the yard.

Several times the creature, wearing a leather mask that covered the left side of his face, charged the wall, flailing its arms and pleading to be left alone. It would be three weeks before the creature claimed its name again. "I am Lazarus, your neighbor."

Sarah dumped a bucket of cold water over Lazarus' head while he squatted in a washtub outside the house. He cupped his hand, ladling some water from the basin and held it under his nose. "What... is... this?" he croaked .

"Myrrh, to kill the stench."

Lazarus slept in a lean-to that had once been his tool shed. At first he tried to accustom himself to living inside the house. It was no use. He was haunted by the spectre of his past existence lingering in the corners. He went through the motions of the living without passion. He slept but felt no need to rest. He ate but lacked the ability to distinguish vinegar from honey.

26

For hours every day Lazarus explored the work yard. He searched for any object, any relic in the cluttered enclosure which would help him to define who he was in the past so that he could learn to be that person again. The implements of his trade were scattered throughout the yard. A chisel, balanced precariously on a slab of granite, gathered dust. A hammer, the head of which was securely attached to its shaft by a band of tin, leaned against the base of the stone. A pillar of marble, partially carved in the shape of a Menorah, dwarfed all the other virgin blocks of granite and marble. The seven-branched candelabrum had been commissioned by a wealthy man in Jerusalem. The Menorah had been abandoned before its completion. The stonecutter had died, and along with him, the project.

Sarah poured another pail of water over Lazarus and handed him a wedge of pumice. Lazarus scraped the hard ash across his flesh. A gaggle of children's faces reappeared at the top of the wall. They taunted him. His presence provided the single form of entertainment in the village, a transitory relief from the monotony of youth. Worse than the children were the parents who came to chase their offspring away from the wall. Generally, Lazarus managed to find privacy under the lean-to. But on those occasions where he was not swift enough to make it into his refuge, a chorus of horror-stricken voices assaulted him. He froze wherever he was standing and stared in astonishment at the women in the crowd who held up bits of polished blue stones while others sprinkled salt around the outside of the wall. Bred on old wives' tales, the women laboured under the conviction that the fiend would not dare to cross the line of salt for fear of being hurled back into the abyss.

Sarah positioned Lazarus' leather mask so that its peephole was over his empty eye socket. She handed him an almond-shaped rock. "It took me all week to find one the right size but I think it will do." A turquoise eyeball had been painted on its white surface. She stood back to admire her work. "Let's see how their blue stones work against this."

Lazarus gritted his teeth and pressed the rock into his eye socket with the flat of his thumb. "Rachel, bring me a robe, please."

27

His wife's soft chanting drifted through the open door. "Our Father Who art in heaven, hallowed be Thy name…"

Sarah trembled, listening to Rachel's pitiful tune, and held up a clean yard of white cloth.

"Give us this day our daily bread…"

"Jeshua taught it to her." Lazarus took the cloth from his mother and wrapped it around his head.

"I know." Sarah tucked the ends of the cloth under the bottom of the turban her son had created. "The poor girl has been repeating it non-stop ever since he left."

"Forgive us our trespasses as we forgive those who trespass against us and lead us not into temptation. For Thine is the kingdom, the power and the glory forever and ever!"

"Amen," the old woman said as she walked to the house. Rachel held out a robe from the open doorway. Sarah brought the garment to Lazarus. The wet cloth wrapped around his lower body clung to his loins. He slipped the robe over his head.

"Holy, Holy, Holy is His name," Rachel blurted out.

Lazarus picked up a wooden mallet from beside the tub. He hurled it at the side of the house. "After listening to that noise for two months, is it any wonder that the villagers hate us?"

Sarah ambled over to the house and poked her finger into the crater the mallet had made in the wall. "Destroying a perfectly good tool doesn't resolve a thing." She groaned as she bent over to retrieve the head of the mallet.

Lazarus turned his back on the house. "She refuses to get within three feet of me."

"This comes as a surprise to you?"

"She's responsible for bringing me back. All I ask is that she acknowledge my existence."

Sarah pressed Lazarus' hand to her cheek. "The smell of the grave hangs over you." She gathered up the soap and pumice and tossed them into her pail. The singing stopped. Rachel emerged from the house wearing a hooded white gown. She stared into the sun. A bird flew across the sky. She lifted her arm, tracking its flight with her finger.

Sarah pulled down Rachel's head. "You'll go blind, girl, looking into the sun like that."

"Bless you, Mother, for those who show mercy and kindness will surely inherit the kingdom of heaven." Rachel kissed Sarah. "He who raises the dead and sits on the right hand of God promises this."

"Damn your Messiah," Lazarus snarled. "I'd like to drag the bastard back here to smell me, his miracle, and listen to your blathering."

"How dare you! He is the Christ and I am his bride."

Sarah squatted on her haunches and drew a line in the dirt. "Don't pay any heed to that bride stuff. We were together the whole time he was here. Nothing happened."

Lazarus' knees popped when he joined the old woman. "Her sisters convinced her, long before I died, that to be worthy when he calls, his followers must be clean in mind, spirit and body."

"Damn mystics, if they're not telling you to go into the desert and eat bugs they're trying to get into your bed," Sarah said, glancing over her shoulder at Eli and Jacob as they marched up to the wall.

Lazarus got up to conceal himself under the lean-to. "I don't have that kind of need anymore."

Eli jammed his hand into a bag suspended from a string around his shoulder. "Crawl out of your filthy den so we can send you back to hell." He pulled out a fistful of salt, held his palm up to his mouth and blew the salt Sarah and Rachel's way. "First we'll deal with the ghoul's bitches."

A wooden crate sailed across the yard. Lazarus surfaced from under the tool shed carrying a rock chisel. Sarah threw herself in front of him to prevent him from reaching the wall. She locked her hands together and used her forearms to steer him back to the shed.

"We have to stay out of people's way. If they don't see you they may fear you, but at least they can't hurt you."

Eli stalked them on the outside of the enclosure, intoning the Shema in a voice so loud that it could be heard throughout the village. He threw a fistful of salt at Lazarus.

Sarah pushed Lazarus back under the lean-to. "We can't afford to cause trouble."

Rachel sang, "Blessed are the meek for they shall inherit the earth."

# 4

The appearance of two strangers in Bethany sent tremors of panic through the populace. The outsiders were dressed in the same white robes as the sorcerer who only two months before had wrought his obscene miracle on the drab village's outskirts.

The villagers responded to the strangers' inquiry of "Where is the home of Lazarus?" with locked jaws. On more than one encounter the individual being questioned licked his thumb and pressed it to his forehead to counter the evil eye.

Ultimately, it was the raucous presence of the children outside the wall which guided them to the stonecutter's dwelling. The elder of the two travellers, Judas, a reed-thin man with hands like a woman's, rapped on the door. He winced and blew on his knuckles after each knock.

On receiving no answer he called his companion and stood to the side. The honey-coloured young man, a descendent of the original seed of Canaan, hammered on the rough wood with the side of his fist.

The door whined on its hinges as it opened slightly. A yellowish eye peeked out at them. Judas craned his neck and looked through the crack. Above the shrivelled head of the old woman he saw Rachel crouching in a corner singing, "Rejoice for sorrow will be no more. On the judgement day we will be restored."

"Go away! Leave us in peace," Sarah demanded.

Judas cleared his throat. "Sister, we have come a long way to visit this place."

His arm arced to take in the horizon. "Show us the miracle that was performed here."

Sarah rolled the corner of her lip over her two good teeth. "There is no miracle here; leastwise, one that's worth visiting."

Judas rubbed the top of his bald dome. "We're not here to gawk. We're followers of Jeshua. We've come to confirm the miracle for his other disciples."

"Damn your master and all his toadies!" Sarah slammed the door. "Come, Simon, the answers we seek are not to be found here."

After a few minutes had passed Sarah peeked out of the window slot. The toadies had not moved far from the house.

They stopped a teenage boy who was on his way to join his friends at the wall and gave him a coin. The boy flipped his head at the hills. With his finger he drew a map in the sand to indicate the direction they should take to reach the caves. It was clear to see that the boy was sending them in the most roundabout way imaginable.

When Judas and Simon were out of sight Sarah left the house. She trudged to the work yard, pushed open the gate and walked behind the unfinished stone Menorah. "Men were here looking for you. They're his followers."

Lazarus rose from behind the grave monument. He strode to a pile of broken stones and picked up a five-pound sledgehammer. "I want to ask them about their Master."

He swung his hammer at the gate, reduced it instantly to kindling, and jogged toward the hills, pausing only once to scowl at the children. They stampeded when he ripped off his mask. He cast a death grin at them. "Good," he said to himself. It had been over two months since Lazarus emerged from his tomb. At that time he was unaware of his surroundings. Yet he held vivid memories of three painful treks he had made to the caves during his first existence.

Three times he had climbed the hill to bury his nameless children, nameless because none of them survived beyond a month. Each infant's death affirmed Rachel's faith in divine providence, driving her in search of God's face among the people. Each cold body cradled in her arms, pressed against her milk-swollen breasts, hastened to sever her from the dreadful reality of life in the here and now and sent her chasing a vision of a better place in the hereafter. Her sisters' arrival with the news of a humble carpenter who stilled the waters, exorcised devils, and moved the masses to renounce their wickedness convinced Rachel that he was the Messiah she craved. Perhaps if she trusted in him indiscriminately, he would bestow the only gift that mattered, life to her babies.

Despite his mother's protests, Lazarus had given in to Rachel's pleas. He allowed her to go with Mary to listen to the Rabbi deliver his message to a gathering of people by the Sea of Galilee. When she returned with stories of the Teacher feeding five thousand with a few loaves of bread and a basket of fish, Lazarus tried to humour her, even coax a smile from her. "Did you bring me back any leftovers?" After her pilgrimage to the sermon on the mount, Rachel withdrew further from Lazarus. Their bodies never touched again.

Lazarus stood at the base of the hills and scanned them for some point of recognition. He started his ascent, arriving at the summit before the two strangers. Their trip had been delayed further by some men in the village who insisted that they explain why they were asking so many questions about the stonecutter. Judas managed to persuade the peasants that they had been sent to Bethany by the Sanhedrin. The mention of the high religious council filled the villagers with awe. What Judas told the men had a measure of truth to it. Lazarus' resurrection had, indeed, caught the attention of the Sanhedrin and fomented bitter, angry debates among its priestly members.

Lazarus stopped to inspect a cave. As he conducted his search he discovered a strip of cloth. He picked up the cloth and held it to his nose. His own mouldy aroma permeated it. Lazarus wadded up the stinking rag and tucked it inside his robe, a memento of his unwanted awakening from a dreamless sleep, then dropped to all fours and squeezed through the narrow opening of the tomb.

In the black interior of the cave Lazarus was able to see as well as if not better than he did in daylight. The warmth emanating from spiders, snakes, and the odd rat scurrying about showed up as pulsating red silhouettes. Objects possessing no life glowed a dawn blue. He closed his eyes, trying to remember when Jeshua's voice had reached him. He remembered being alive and sick, darkness descending, and nothing after that until he crawled into the burning sunlight. He had re-entered the world with no more understanding the second time around than he had the first time. Reason, it seemed, was not part of Hashem's great plan. He had lurched out of the cave only to be abandoned by the person who had given him life.

"Live, die, live, and then what?" He was never very good at answering riddles, much less ones of such profound significance. He was a stonecutter. There were no mysteries in his occupation. Cleave clean and steady and the stone survived. Veer one inch off the mark and the stone was finished, good only for throwing at whores and adulterers. It was simple. A simple rule for a simple man. All rules were simple if you followed them without questioning.

He fasted when it was time to fast and feasted when it was time to feast, because that's what he was supposed to do. No mystery. There was no need to ask why. Hashem says it is so, so it is so.

"But this..." a mousy sneeze from outside the cave brought Lazarus out of his meditation and to his feet.

"Keep it down, Simon. We'll have a lot of explaining to do if someone finds us here."

Lazarus crept up to the entrance of the cave and looked out through the crawl-space. Judas and Simon were busy pulling away armfuls of slag to enlarge the opening. When the hole was large enough they hunched their shoulders and lowered their heads, blindly feeling their way through the narrow aperture. Lazarus retreated to the blackness of the cave. As the men moved to the centre of the chamber, the aura surrounding them grew brighter. Simon's hair hung past the middle of his back, tied with a leather strip.

"A Nazarite," Lazarus thought.

The thin, bald man, unaware of Lazarus' presence, barked at Simon, "If you had remembered to bring a torch we could have done some real investigating in here."

"Be quiet, Judas. It was your idea to come here, not mine."

Lazarus bounced a pebble across the cave.

"Whoa, what's that?" Judas cupped his hand over his eyebrows, peering into the darkness. Simon rushed forward, colliding with Lazarus. He screamed, then fainted. Judas bolted from the cave.

Lazarus picked up the young man and carried him into the sunlight. He propped him against a boulder. "Stop that!" Lazarus yelled when he felt a whack across his shoulders.

Judas brandished a leafy stick. "Stand back or I'll —"

Lazarus grabbed the stick from his assailant. "Or you'll what?" Judas' face receded into his thick beard.

Lazarus pressed the stick to his mouth and bit off the leaves one by one. "You're trespassing." He pulled out the sledgehammer hidden inside his robe. "This is my cave."

"We should have asked permission before entering," Judas gasped. He placed his hands on his companion and jostled him into consciousness.

"It wasn't a dream," Simon bawled as he scrambled to his feet. "He's truly horrible."

Lazarus spit the masticated leaves at the men. "I'm not horrible. I'm a damned miracle."

"Calm down. This is Lazarus. He wouldn't hurt the Master's disciples."

"The Master?" Lazarus gagged on the title Judas had bestowed on the mystic.

"Yes, Jeshua. You wouldn't harm the followers of the man responsible for bringing you back to your family."

"Harm you? Hell, I'm going to eat you."

Simon made a show of reclaiming his courage. "If you are going to kill us then get it over with."

"This is my cave," Lazarus said, dropping the branch. "Tell me quickly what you want and get out of here."

"We had to see if it was true," Judas started to explain.

"It's more than we'd hoped for." Simon interrupted Judas in mid-sentence. "It's a godsend. If only we can convince him to do it again."

"That's enough." Judas placed his hand over his companion's mouth.

Lazarus pulled him away from Simon. "Go on with what you were saying."

Simon's eyes glowed when he related his fantasy. "Imagine if Jeshua could resurrect our greatest warriors and heroes like David, Samson and Abner to fight the Romans. That would frighten them back where they came from."

Lazarus failed to conceal the derision in his voice. "Why is that everyone who follows your Rabbi sounds as batty as my wife?"

"Simon and I are devotees of Jeshua," Judas said. "He has proven himself to be much more than just your run-of-the-mill teacher. He may very well be the Messiah we have all been waiting for."

"Maybe to you he is," Simon interjected. "He lacks the fortitude to confront our enemies head on. He'd rather sit around burbling about love thy neighbor and peace on earth than liberating our land from pagans who mock our God."

Judas patted Simon's head. "He's a good boy."

"How many of you are there?" Lazarus asked.

"How many what?"

"Followers of this so-called Messiah."

Simon and Judas conferred with one another. Judas replied, "Last count around twelve." He failed to mention that it was not a cohesive group. Dissension was the rule rather than the exception among Jeshua's followers. Simon and Judas leaned toward the camp of the Zealots. They were convinced if they could get Jeshua to assume leadership, to take charge, he could rally an army around him to purge the land of Hashem's enemies, Jews and Romans alike. Unfortunately,

Jeshua refused to get involved in such mundane matters. Judas and Simon were sick of hearing him proclaim to all who would listen that his kingdom was not of this earth. *"Render unto Caesar that which is Caesar's and unto God that which is God's."*

Lazarus clapped his hands to get their attention. "Get out of here. Go back and tell your friends that you've seen me."

Simon sprinted down the hill. "Some Zealot," Lazarus said.

"He's young. He'll learn," Judas replied.

"I'm older and I haven't learned anything. I don't even know what the question is, much less the answer that would explain why I've been brought back."

"Maybe there is nothing to learn. Maybe the answer is the same one that Job received."

"Leave."

As Judas walked away he peeked inside the cave. "Do you come here every day to sleep?"

"I'm a man, not a ghoul. This is the first time I've returned since I was resurrected."

"There will be others, you know."

"I'm sure all of his disciples will visit this place."

"No, I mean others who will come to disprove that a miracle actually happened, who will set out to level the Teacher and anyone associated with him. There is already talk that you are nothing more than a familiar conjured up by a warlock."

"If it hadn't happened to me, I'd probably agree with them."

"When they come, they will set out to destroy you so that they can destroy him."

"Let them come."

"One is on his way already, a Jew by birth, a Roman citizen by decree. He despises the Teacher. It's rumoured his hatred goes back to when he was twelve and studying in the Temple. It seems that another twelve-year-old astounded the priests with his knowledge of Torah. He so outshone their prized pupil that the boy never forgave Jeshua."

37

"That's a long time to carry a grudge."

"When a people has been waiting over a thousand years for a Messiah, what's one man's grudge against another?"

"I don't know. I've just started cultivating mine."

After Simon and Judas were out of sight, Lazarus re-entered his tomb. The darkness embraced him. The scent of the damp earth underfoot and the green moss clinging to the walls of the cave aroused him. He lay down where he'd been displayed as the main course for the rats and vermin that infested the cave. The cave floor was cool, soothing. He was tired. He had not really slept since his return. He stretched himself out on top of the table, closed his eyes and tried to dream his death. "Perhaps," he questioned as he attempted to dissolve his consciousness, "to be alive is the nightmare of the dead?"

There was no voice from the other side exhorting him, "Lazarus, die." He lifted his head and spread his feet apart. Between them, he saw the fingernail sliver of the sun disappear below the horizon. The sun vanished, leaving a sky the colour of a pomegranate bleeding over the hills.

# 5

It was dark when Lazarus returned to his village. Once he was certain Rachel was asleep, he entered the house and stood inside the threshold. He attempted to distinguish her scent from the ever-present miasma surrounding him. From behind a curtain dividing the hut he heard Rachel's breathing. It was thick and rapid. She was the pulse, the force which prevented the dwelling from crumbling into dust. He wanted to hold her, feel her skin against his, his lips on her lips. But this was out of the realm of possibility. His breath smelled of the tomb. His lips, tight and drawn across his teeth in a sardonic grin, would scrape her raw, turning what was once an act of pleasure into one of penance. It was one matter to live with a miracle, another entirely to make love to one.

Sunlight crept into the house. The night was short, shorter than he wished. Lazarus felt the weight of a hand on his shoulder.

His mother stood behind him. "Have you been up all night?"

"Night, day, it's all the same to me."

Rachel entered the room. She placed a tallit over her head and began to wrap the leather straps of the tefillin around her forearm.

"What is she up to now?" Sarah asked.

Rachel recited the berakha adding at the end, "Blessed be those women who abandon their nature to serve Your Son."

"This has gone far enough!" Lazarus tried to remove her tefillin.

"Leave the girl alone. She has lost her mind."

"It's not crazy to worship the Son of God," Rachel responded.

"Where are you getting this stuff!" Lazarus demanded.

Rachel cocked her head to the side and tapped her temple with her index finger. "Jeshua tells me things."

"How come I can't hear him?"

"He whispers His secrets to me."

Lazarus felt his heart grow cold. "Like what?"

"He's come to liberate women from the oppression of Moses."

Sarah took Rachel's hand and guided her to the fire pit beyond Lazarus' reach. Rachel was mesmerized by the glowing coals of the fire. She hummed and swayed from side to side, oblivious to the world about her. Even the repeated thud of rocks striking the walls of the house failed to bring her out of her trance.

Sarah got up to investigate the noise from outside. When she opened the door a rock the size of a goose egg sailed past her head and smashed a clay pot. "What the —" She rushed out in time to see three teenage boys flee. "Go ahead and run. I recognise you, Dov, Ari, Natan," she yelled after them.

Lazarus nudged Sarah out of the doorway. He picked up a stone and threw it. He was surprised at how much his accuracy had improved since his return to the living. The rock struck one of the boys between his shoulder blades, knocking him down. The other two boys interrupted their getaway. Draping their friend's arms over their shoulders they dragged him between them as they continued their flight.

Lazarus picked up another stone. Perhaps he could nail one more of the little bastards who tormented him and his family.

"Put down the rock," Sarah ordered. "Things are bad enough without you pelting the village darlings."

The boys returned with their fathers and several other men. They huddled together about twenty yards away, and looked up from their conference at Lazarus. One youth lifted his robe to display a conspicuous bruise in the middle of his back to the men.

Sarah pulled Lazarus into the house. She barred the door behind her and leaned against it. A rain of stones showered the door. Lazarus tore across the room to a battered tool chest, lifted its lid, and took out an iron rod tapered at one end into a chisel head.

"Blessed are the peacemakers: for they shall be called the children of God," Rachel proclaimed and smiled beatifically at Sarah. "Have you heard the good news?"

"News?" Sarah scowled at Rachel. "The news is that people think you're possessed."

"I am possessed, possessed of the truth."

Lazarus' fingers tightened around the shaft of the rod when Jacob bellowed from outside, "Give us the demon!"

"Don't go. Think of Rachel." Sarah blocked Lazarus' way to the door. "She's got no one. Even her own mother condemns her."

"My mother." Rachel pronounced the word like a profanity. "She saw Him and denied Him. She that loves her father or mother more than the Master is not worthy of Him."

"Be still." Sarah pinched Rachel's cheek. "Girl, you'll need all your wits if you're going to come through this in one piece."

"Come on! What are we afraid of? Let's drag them out here." Eli's exhortation was backed up by a cheer of approval from the mob he had gathered around him.

Sarah sank onto her stool when a torrent of stones shook the dwelling. "So much for the housewarming."

Lazarus grasped the butt end of the rod like a war club. "Jacob!" he yelled, "you used to call me friend."

"The friend I had is dead and buried."

"Burn the house to the ground with everyone in it," Eli piped up.

Lazarus dropped his head and charged across the room like a bull. The door exploded off its hinges. Jacob stood a few feet away holding a torch. The crowd surrounding Jacob scattered when Lazarus swung the chisel. His blow knocked the torch out of his old friend's hand. Lazarus drove the head of the rod into the earth at the mill-stone owner's feet.

"Is this what you want?"

Jacob held his ground without flinching. "This is what the law of Moses demands."

"That's right," Eli urged the crowd. "Witches and their offspring must be excised and their bodies consumed by fire."

Jacob dipped into his purse, pulled out a fistful of salt and threw it in Lazarus' face.

Lazarus grasped the purse and jerked. The thong securing it around Jacob's neck broke. He licked his fingertips, dipped them into the wallet, withdrawing them coated with salt. "What a waste." He held the purse upside down and shook it empty.

Eli tried to incite the mob action. "There's only one of him. Let's take him."

"There are seven of us." A Roman centurion used his shield to clear a path through the middle of the crowd. He was followed by three soldiers marching abreast. Behind them walked four men dressed in purple robes, wearing the white-and-goldtrimmed headdresses of the Sanhedrin, the Jewish high court. Next in the procession were three more Romans carrying staffs from which flew banners emblazoned with war eagles.

"Make way, make way," a shrill voice commanded. Through the ranks of the soldiers and priests slipped a wispy little man. He stamped his foot when he finally made it to the head of the group. He dangled his hands from his wrists in front of him, fluttering them at the villagers. "Shoo, shoo. Get back with you."

"This is no concern of Rome's," Jacob said.

The man placed his hand behind his ear. "Excuse me. Did you say something?"

Jacob eyed the soldiers nervously. "I told you that what is going on here is none of Rome's affair."

"Ah yes, I see. Thank you." The man reached up, snatched Jacob by his beard and yanked his face down to him. "See those fellows standing over there?" He twisted Jacob's head by the beard toward the priests. "It is up to them to see whose concern all this is." He released Jacob. Two soldiers hauled him away.

The wispy man pressed his fingertips to his lips. "Oh, my. Is this what I've come all this way to see? This creature is hardly worthy of being called a miracle. It looks more like a unfinished bowel movement."

"I'm Lazarus."

"It speaks." The man played with the medallions hanging from the ropes of gold chain draped around his neck. His simple Hebrew robe was embellished by a crimson sash falling over one shoulder and silver bracelets jingling on his delicate wrists. His hairstyle was that of a Roman patrician, bangs trimmed to fall in a fringe across his forehead.

The man looked away from Lazarus when the two soldiers returned. They raised their arms and pounded their leather breastplates. He returned their gesture half-heartedly. The priests formed a circle around Lazarus. The man placed the end of his thumb in his mouth, sucking on its tip a moment before speaking. "Take him into his house," he ordered the centurion whose sword was unsheathed. "No one enters or leaves until I make arrangements for the inquisition. I may need some of your men to help me set up the tent. If there is enough time, you might even find your way clear to asking the garrison commander to come by and look at the tent. It's one of my better models."

"I'm a Roman centurion. No Jew will order me around like a house servant."

"It is not a Jew ordering you. When I speak, Marcus, it is Caesar speaking. When I speak to them," he pointed at the priests, "it is Herod who talks."

Marcus slashed the air in defiance before putting his sword away. "Take this thing inside." He grabbed Lazarus and tried to sling him toward his men. Lazarus did not budge. His hand sought out the proper weight of the chisel.

"Please, don't make a scene." The odd little man peeked around Lazarus and waved at Sarah and Rachel, who stood inside the doorway. "Make sure those two remain with him. I'll have to call on them for testimony."

"What testimony?" Lazarus asked.

"Your petty little village has become quite famous since your return. So famous, in fact, the Sanhedrin has asked me to conduct an investigation to determine if you are truly alive or if you are merely an animated cadaver. Having no precedent for this sort of thing, I am here to weigh the physical facts against the metaphysical evidence."

"Who are you to make this determination?"

"I am Saul of Tarsus."

# 6

The task of watching over Lazarus was assigned to Flavius. His youth and inexperience in battle resulted in his having to assume the most ignoble of duties, acting as a turnkey at the behest of a Jew.

For over a week Flavius had escorted his wards through the gauntlet of people and beyond the limits of the town to tend to their bodily functions.

"How many days does it take before your council meets to render a decision?" Flavius' propensity to pose meaningless questions irritated Lazarus as much as it did the boy's fellow soldiers.

"I don't know. This is my first time for this sort of thing."

"We've been here since..." The soldier started counting off the days on his hand.

"Put away your fingers. We haven't picked up a day since you last counted."

"Oh well, at least we won't starve," Flavius said.

It was true. Saul saw to it to that they were well fed. Meats, breads and fruits, which before their incarceration they could only have dreamt of, were sent over each morning.

Sarah plucked a ripe date from its plate. She crammed the sweet fruit into her mouth. With her few remaining teeth she ground it into paste. She dipped a piece of bread into a bowl of honey, devoured it without chewing, and peeked at the young soldier from the corner of her eye. When she was satisfied he could not see her, she scooped up a handful of dates, squirrelling them away under her robe.

Lazarus refused to take part in the feast. "They gorge chickens before they wring their necks," he grumbled.

Rachel passed through the curtain into the living section of the hovel. "Fear not, for are you any less than the birds in the sky and flowers in the field over which He watches?" She picked up the wash tub, carried it back with her and pulled the curtain closed. Behind the thin divider Rachel filled the tub, then disrobed.

Flavius was painfully aware of the presence of the young woman bathing behind the almost transparent curtain. Her naked silhouette was projected on the fabric like a shadow puppet he had once seen in a mountebank's show.

"Girl, put your gown on!" Sarah spewed a mouthful of date pulp.

Flavius knew that the barbarians who inhabited this land were fanatically opposed to any show of flesh, any hint of sexuality. Though he tried not to, he cast a longing glance in the direction of the curtain.

Rachel dipped a sponge into the tub and caressed her naked torso. Her nipples grew erect as she touched them. She lifted one arm above her head and ran the sponge along her side. "The womb of woman will become the temple of humanity," she chanted.

Lazarus lifted his head from his chest. Though the leather mask concealed half his face, his one good eye contained enough sorrow to drown the nation. Lazarus ripped down the curtain and threw it over Rachel. He resisted the urge to swaddle her in his arms and beg forgiveness whatever sin he had committed which Adonai saw fit to punish by driving Rachel into madness. Retreating to a corner, Lazarus turned his back on his wife. Of all the emotions to resurface, love was the most excruciating.

Sarah offered her hand to Rachel and led her to a chair. "Look all you want, boy," she scolded Flavius. "Looking is all she's good for. She's not right in the mind."

Rachel shut her eyes and resumed her chanting. "My body is an empty vessel awaiting His spirit to enter it."

"Imagine, a Vestal Virgin in these parts," Flavius said.

Lazarus sat down at the feet of the soldier. "There is no place for women who deny their nature in our world."

"I wish I could say the same about Rome. Our priests consecrate our best-looking women to Hestia. It's dumb luck that Saturn's only daughter would have to be a virgin. But it's our belief and it has served us well."

"Once a people abandons its beliefs, it ceases to be a people."

The Jew's words haunted the soldier. They reminded him of his father, who had spent the last years of his life cursing Rome's decline. "Boy, as long as we were content to farm the land and practice the old beliefs we were strong, or at least we were until we allowed the religions and practices of the nations we've conquered to pollute us." Flavius stuck his hand into a pouch attached to his girdle and removed a strip of meat the texture of worn shoe leather. "Here, eat."

Lazarus shook his head. "I can't take it. It is—"

"I know. It's against your bloody laws." Flavius ground his teeth on the strip of meat, tugging at it until he tore off a piece. "I can't wait until my duty is over. When I return home I never want to hear about, see, or listen to a Jew again."

"There is no one stopping you from leaving," Sarah snarled and placed her hand on Rachel's arm to stop her from rocking.

Flavius rose to his feet and slapped his hand against the hilt of his sword. "The truth is we were invited here by Herod. He was sick of the endless petty wars between the religious sects in your country. Even if we are unable to bring you civilization, we can still bring you peace, whether you want it or not."

"Ah," Sarah groaned. "What do you know? You take the word of a man who sleeps with his brother's wife as an invitation."

"I can't believe I'm having this discussion with a barbarian. You're so backward that you can't even accept a heroic occurrence when you see one." Flavius looked at Lazarus. "In Rome this man would be revered."

"Come again?" Sarah stuck her finger into her ear and pretended to clean it out. "Hashem knows I care for this man. He is not only my son, he is the only being I know who is more alone than I am. But a heroic occurrence? Not by anyone's definition. My son is here because some megalomaniac brought him back from Sheol."

The thick muscles of Flavius' neck stood out on its side. "You people are so ignorant. You deserved to be conquered. Our holy writings and the stories of our heroes are full of tales of men who have crossed the Styx and returned to the land of the living. Your religion lacks imagination. It is content to worship one god because you are too crude, too simple, to create a great history for yourselves."

"Hashem, not man, creates history," Sarah said.

"It's useless talking to you, old woman. Look at this man. He is your Aeneas."

"I'm just a stonecutter." Lazarus removed the soldier's spear from the corner and handed it to Flavius. "Act soldierly, I hear someone coming."

A boot kick toppled the door balanced precariously in the doorway. "Stand tall!" Marcus barked. Saul and his entourage of ancient judges entered the hut behind a guard of three soldiers.

"Come out of the shadows," Saul commanded. Lazarus stepped forward. Twirling the belt of his robe, Saul waved its tasselled end at one of the Sanhedrin members. The priest, circling Lazarus warily, poked at his stomach and studied his face. Outside, a crowd started to congregate. The curious villagers peeked through the window slots and milled about the open doorway. Lazarus remained expressionless. The priest walked back to Saul, whispered in his ear. Saul nodded. They were unaware that Lazarus detected every movement, every sound in the room, no matter how slight.

Saul handed a tent maker's seaming needle to Marcus. The centurion thrust the needle into the middle of the glowing coals of the fire pit. Saul slapped at the flies circling his head with a fan painted with the image of two infants suckling a she-wolf. "Get on with it, man, we don't have all day."

Marcus held the white-hot implement near Lazarus' cheek. Before the metal could sear his flesh, Lazarus clamped his hand around the

Roman's wrist and squeezed. The centurion's fingers slowly unfurled like the fronds of fern. The needle fell to the floor. The sound of the soldiers unsheathing their swords filled the room. Lazarus shoved Marcus away and retrieved the needle. He jabbed it through the thick vein of his forearm. "Does this satisfy you? I bleed." The blood spurted, puddling at his feet.

All the soldiers except for Flavius fell on Lazarus. They slammed him face first into the wall. Lazarus did not struggle. His arms went limp as his hands were bound behind him. Marcus seized the ends of the rope, planted his foot in the small of Lazarus' back, pulling at the cord until it cut into his wrists.

"Take him to the tent," Saul ordered.

Marcus sneered at Flavius. "Since you don't have the stomach to do a man's work, you bring the women."

The villagers were prepared for the prisoners' emergence from the house. Tidy piles of stones and dung lay at their feet. They took care not to hit the soldiers. "Whore, witch, monster," and other insults and invectives accompanied every projectile that struck its target.

The procession stopped in front of a large blue-and-white striped tent. Rachel's eyes were fixed on a banner bearing the ensign of Rome flying from the top of the tent. She preached over the noise of the mob, "And the King shall answer and say unto them, Verily I say unto you, inasmuch as you have done it unto the least of these My brethren, you have done it unto Me."

Flavius placed his hand on Rachel's shoulder. She slipped from under his touch, dropped to one knee and spread her arms out in front of the crowd. "And these shall go away into everlasting punishment: but the righteous into life eternal."

The women in the crowd held up bits of blue stone to ward off the evil eye. Rachel laughed. "That will do you no good. You will still enter Sheol damned."

An ancient man exited the tent dressed in a purple robe trimmed in silver and gold. "Perhaps there is truth to this, but now it is time for you to enter your place of judgement."

49

The silver-haired ecclesiastic's bearing was that of a person accustomed to having people pay him homage. A square breastplate hung from around his neck inscribed with the words *"Hear O Israel: the Lord our God, the Lord is one."* On his head he wore a white mitre identifying him as one of the select few allowed to penetrate the innermost sanctum of the Temple. His waist-length beard brushed the side of Rachel's face when he leaned over to give her his hand. She stood, smoothed her gown and combed her fingers through her hair. "Treat these women with dignity when you deliver them to their seats," the priest warned Flavius.

Saul kneaded the fabric of the tent flap between his thumb and index finger as the soldiers shuffled Lazarus and the women past him. "So strong that it can withstand the worst wind, yet so fine that it breathes like a baby," he whispered, stroking the side of his face with the material.

"Saul," the voice of the ancient priest thundered. "Quit admiring your handicraft and get up here."

Saul bowed, folding his arms across his chest. "I'm sorry, Lord Gamaliel. Sometimes I forget to separate my trade concerns from my religious duties."

Gamaliel snorted and gestured with his walking staff at a long cedar table. Behind the table three high-backed chairs stood on either side of a massive winged ebony throne gilded with mock gold foil and encrusted with paste jewels. The old man stood behind the throne, praying in a voice so low that it sounded like the hum of a bee. When he was finished he faced the throne. "Let the wisdom of Solomon guide our steps. May truth lead to justice and justice be tempered by compassion."

"Amen," Saul responded, bowing three times: once to the East, next to the throne and lastly to Gamaliel.

"Stand them up," Gamaliel said. The guards jerked Lazarus and the women to their feet. "Do you know why you are here?"

Sarah coughed. "I know if a Temple high priest comes all this way to our nothing town, it can't be good."

Gamaliel leaned over to confer with his fellow tribunal members. Saul shook his head emphatically. "The women must be present. His return from the grave may have been through their black intervention."

Gamaliel's head wobbled on his spindly neck. "Young woman, how long have you known this old woman?"

"As long as she has known me."

The villagers crammed into the tent exploded in laughter when someone said, "Bitch, from the looks of things you'll be parting company at the same time."

Sarah twisted her head around. She set her eyes on Eli. "Your jokes are no better than your baking. They are as flat as your bread and twice as dry."

"Oh yeah, well this will be the last thing you taste from my hands." The baker held a rock above his head.

Saul flicked his fan at Eli. The baker yelped when a soldier snatched him by his hair and hauled him outside the tent.

"This is a serious matter. I demand you show a little decorum." Gamaliel waited for the noise to die down before continuing the inquest. "Old woman, what part did you play in this abomination?"

"I played a very small part. I gave him birth."

"Young woman, did you summon Jeshua here?"

"Does man have the power to call forth the sun?" Rachel answered.

"Please, my child, be careful what you say," Gamaliel cautioned.

Lazarus stood up. "My Lord, for seven days we have been kept prisoners in our own house. If I have committed a crime, other than being the victim of what some call a miracle, let me know what it is so that I can plead guilty and be over with it."

Saul's face was scorched with anger. "Idiot, you are here as evidence of a crime against nature. The man you call the Messiah is the one who should be on trial."

"I never called him that," Lazarus responded. "I never called him period."

Gamaliel pushed Saul back into his chair. "We have been sent here by the Sanhedrin to determine if you are truly alive or if you are the physical manifestation of the power of evil. We have brought your wife and your mother here to see if they were simply observers of this event or if they are in some way responsible."

"Suffer not a witch to live," Saul interrupted.

"You overdressed Roman flunky. I'm no more a witch than you are a man. My offense is that I had the misfortune to love my children and outlive them."

"It's not up to you decide the nature of your transgression."

Gamaliel lifted his staff over his head with both hands and brought it down on the edge of the table. "Be quiet!" His rage quickly subsided as he collapsed into his throne.

The silence was broken by Marcus. "Damn Jews. If I was Caesar, I'd wait for them to kill each other off and then march in and sweep up what remains."

Saul swished his hand in front of his face. "No one asked for your political opinion, Marcus. But you can trust I will enlighten your captain with it when we return to the garrison."

"I have a judgement to render." Gamaliel scooted his chair away from the table and slowly rose to his feet. "This man is either truly the result of a miracle or he is the product of the dark arts. These women are either simply witnesses to an act of God, or are Satan's hand-maidens. Without knowing which is which, I can pass no sentence."

"Lunacy! You failed to render a proper judgement," Saul inveighed.

"Don't question me." Gamaliel's voice dropped like an anvil. "This is the only judgement I can make. Until which time someone can prove that a miracle has not occurred, I must presume one has occurred. If it came from God, there is no use denying it. If it came from Satan, then there is no use fighting it. Ultimately the resolution to this mystery will come from Hashem alone."

"That's it? That's all you have to say?" Saul sputtered.

"No, there is one more thing. Unbind the prisoner's hands. He and the women are to go free."

Marcus looked at Saul for confirmation. Saul slumped in his chair. Resigned to the decision, he told Lazarus, "You and your women are free to go, but as a liaison between Rome and Judea I reserve the right to say where you are free to go. Until such time as Hashem reveals His verdict, you are banished from this village. Furthermore, you're denied the right to spend more than two weeks in any town you travel through."

Gamaliel slapped the table with an open palm. "Wait, this was not my decree."

"I adhere to the spirit of your decision but as a loyal Roman citizen I must consider the public peace."

"What about my wife and mother?" Lazarus' cavernous voice smothered the conversations that had erupted throughout the tent.

"My decision applies to you. Your women are free to remain here and take their chances with your neighbours." Saul puffed up his chest, releasing his venom in one breathless spray of words. "Perhaps during your travels you can seek out Jeshua. Ask him why he botched the job so terribly in bringing you back to life. If he is truly a miracle worker he should be able to restore you to a better physical representation of your former self. If he can't, not only is he a blasphemer, he's an incompetent."

Sarah took Lazarus' hand. With her other hand she held Rachel, who insisted on making faces at the villagers assembled at the front of the tent.

Rachel wrenched free of Sarah and ran back to the table. "I'll go with him to spread the good news about my Saviour."

"Take care, child," Gamaliel admonished her. "These are dangerous times, and in dangerous times it is sometimes more prudent to keep what is in your heart concealed from those who don't see things the same way you do."

"All the world will come to see the light," Rachel proclaimed.

"And you, will you go with them too?" Gamaliel asked Sarah.

Sarah's bony shoulders rose and fell. "An old woman is entitled to travel before she dies. Besides, someone has to keep an eye on these two to make sure they don't get into trouble."

The crowd closed in on them as they started for the exit. Slaps and kicks marked each one of their steps.

"Let them pass." Marcus signalled his men to force the mob back.

Flavius tugged at Lazarus' sleeve as he walked by him and whispered, "At what time will you leave?"

A rock appeared in the hands of Eli. He had concealed himself outside the tent. Before the rock could crush Lazarus' skull, Flavius' sword sliced through the air, decapitating Eli in one swipe. The baker's head rolled under the feet of the horrified villagers. They trampled one another to escape the spears of the approaching soldiers, kicking the mutilated head in front of them like a ball.

"This is what comes of your saviour." Saul flipped the table over while Gamaliel broke into stunned prayer.

# 7

Lazarus sat inside the doorway with his legs crossed, providing a nest for Sarah to rest her head. He moved aside the blanket covering the hole where the door had once hung and looked outside. A gelatinous sun shimmered over the village, obscuring the bloated bodies of the flies hovering above the dwellings.

By sunset he would be miles away from the blighted remains of his past. Lazarus imagined himself standing on the crest of the highest knoll. Beyond the hills were great cities inhabited by people of whom he'd heard, but had never seen.

Sarah sat up. It was a mother's job to understand what her child was thinking. She would act as an extension of her son, as his sensor, his means of evaluating the new world they would encounter.

"You don't have to follow me, Mother. I can drop you off where people have never heard of me."

"You're my blood. Besides, you'll need intelligent company during your wanderings."

"Rachel will be with me."

"Like I said, you'll need intelligent company."

"The journey will be difficult. Here at least you have friends."

"There is nothing holding me here. All I have are the caves." She patted Lazarus on his knee with a gnarled, liver-spotted hand. "What are you going to say to the carpenter once you find him?"

Lazarus stuck his fingers into his tangled hair and pulled out a louse. He held it up to the light before releasing it. "I'll beg him to restore Rachel's sanity, and then, if he can fix me so that I can walk in daylight again without others recoiling in horror, I'll worship him."

Sarah's pragmatic side surfaced as she realised that come evening she would be gone from the village she had called home for eight decades. "We have to start considering how we're going to live on our journey."

"Live?"

Sarah crossed the room to take an empty goatskin down from its hook. "Well we don't have time to worry about it now." She slung the water bag over her shoulder. "Best tell Rachel to get a move on if we intend to leave today. I'm going to fetch some water for our trip."

Lazarus leaned against the empty door frame. The sun cast Sarah's elongated shadow on the ground as it followed her past the gawking women and children. He called over his shoulder to Rachel. "Get up. We'll be leaving as soon as Mother returns from the well."

"Glory be to Him that—"

He cut Rachel's chant short. "Yeah, I know, Him that was and is and always will be."

"Fear not, for just as our Lord provided for our ancestors in their flight from Pharaoh, she shall provide for us in our flight toward freedom and the holy light." Rachel stood next to Lazarus. Her robe was draped over her arm. She patted her naked breast. "I feel the spirit in here. When I meet with our Saviour, I will tell Him what I have heard so that He can spread the gospel throughout the nations of the world."

Lazarus lacked the energy to confront her madness. "Decide what we are going take with us." He picked a hemp sack off the floor and gave it to her. "Be sure to bring along enough to feed your saviour in case we run into him." He sat in his corner and closed his eyes, felt himself teetering on the edge of sleep for the first time in several days.

"Lazarus!" Sarah's scream jolted him awake. He snatched from the table the curtain that he had ripped down earlier. When he arrived at the well a dozen men had Sarah trapped in the centre of their circle. She was doubled over, covering her head with her arms to shield herself against the fists and kicks aimed at her. Lazarus loaded the blanket with the stones the men had piled nearby. He slung it across his shoulder and warned the men to back off. They failed to withdraw. He attacked, swinging the lethal sling over his head.

Everyone scattered except for Jacob. "It's because of him that we are burying Eli!"

Lazarus continued whirling the blanket above his head, forcing the mob to retreat from Sarah. "Enough's enough! We won't cause you any more problems."

Jacob threw a rock at Lazarus, striking him above the eyebrow. Blood sprayed from Lazarus' forehead. He dropped the blanket and rushed his adversary. Jacob swung at him. Lazarus slipped the blow and trapped Jacob in a choke hold.

Jacob tried to break free but ceased his struggles when Lazarus hissed, "Keep still or I swear I'll rip your head off with my bare hands."

One of the villagers ran up to Lazarus. "Look at his wound." An eerie silence fell over the crowd. The laceration above Lazarus' eyebrow vanished before them.

"Disperse!" The crowd parted when Saul appeared accompanied by Flavius, Marcus and another soldier. He reached up and touched the spot where the rock had struck Lazarus. "Amazing."

"We need to talk." Saul hooked his arm through the crook of Lazarus' elbow and led him away from the well. "Take the old woman back to her house and give her enough provisions to last them three days," he instructed Flavius.

"I've had it with talking. I'm leaving, just as you told me to."

Saul grasped Lazarus' arm and rolled up his sleeve above his elbow. "Amazing, truly amazing. I wonder what Gamaliel's judgement would have been if he had seen this."

From inside his robe Saul pulled out the needle Lazarus had thrust through his arm the day before. He stabbed it with such force into Lazarus' palm that its point came out on the other side of his hand. Anticipating Lazarus' response, Saul rolled away from the stonecutter's hammer-like blow in time to prevent himself from being driven into the earth.

Lazarus' rage increased, but he was prevented from taking a second swipe. Marcus and the remaining soldier spun Lazarus around and kicked him in the middle of his leg. Lazarus collapsed. Marcus yanked Lazarus' head back. The soldier held his sword across his throat. Saul lifted Lazarus' arm by the wrist and pulled the needle out. He waited for the hole in Lazarus' palm to close.

"Incredible. In yesterday's excitement I failed to observe it. If it hadn't been for Marcus recalling the event for me, it would have passed unnoticed. Today's altercation, though unplanned, has confirmed the unbelievable."

Marcus drove his knee into the small of Lazarus' back, sending him sprawling face down in the dirt.

"Help him to his feet," Saul said. Lazarus waved away the soldiers. He stood, clenching his fists as he faced Saul.

"My dear fellow, with your temper things could get increasingly difficult for you as you journey through life. And if your astonishing powers of recuperation are any indication, it is going to be a long life indeed."

"I'm tired of riddles," Lazarus said.

Saul hugged himself as he burst into laughter. "You poor ignorant peasant." He skipped over to Lazarus and tapped him on his forehead. "You really don't understand." Placing his mouth near Lazarus' ear, he confided, "Not only has your master brought you back from the grave, he's endowed you with the power to heal yourself."

"I don't know what Jeshua is, but I do know that he's not my master."

"Devil or saviour, he's done you no favours." Saul placed his fan under Lazarus' chin. "You are marked like Cain. Leave this village today. Avoid the cities. People will seek you out and use you to support their own causes. Rome hates causes. Become a myth. Myths hold no power. Find a place in the desert to hide and, if possible, die there."

"Yesterday you wanted to kill me and today you're giving me advice."

"In our country we have no tomorrows."

The soldiers marched Lazarus to his house. Sarah and Rachel sat on two large bags they had prepared for the trip. Flavius was beside them. "The old woman is in bad shape," he informed his comrades.

"To hell with her," Marcus grunted. "Let's get these people out of here so we can go back to being soldiers, not nursemaids to stinking Jews."

"Can you walk?" Lazarus asked Sarah.

"I'll try."

Flavius threw down his spear. "No, you won't. I'll carry you as far as we are allowed to take you."

"You don't have do this," Lazarus said.

"Yes, I do." As Flavius started off, he marshalled the other soldiers. "Help them with their sacks so we can get this over with and be done with them." He broke into a quick march, setting the pace of the group out of the village.

Lazarus jogged to catch up with Flavius. "You're not like a Roman."

"You're not like a Jew."

"But I am a Jew, more of a Jew than these people who are driving me away."

"And I am a Roman," Flavius replied.

# 8

The hills vanished, giving way to miles of cracked earth and sparse vegetation. Sandstone spires and monolithic blocks of limestone dominated the terrain. The fossilized remains of creatures embedded in rock and scattered across this wasteland divulged a history before Noah's flood.

For three days Lazarus carried Sarah in his arms. "Put me down before I forget how to use my legs," she demanded.

Lazarus spotted a bush large enough to offer some shade and placed her underneath its branches. Rachel brought a goatskin to the old woman. She poured what amounted to little more than a few thimbles of water into a bowl Sarah formed with her cupped hands. Sarah lapped up the liquid puddled in the hollow of her palm. She held out her hands for more water.

Miles away a needle rock pierced a cloud. Lazarus felt the desire to abandon his charges and scale the steeple. The urge to do so quickly faded. His attention returned to the necessity of making it out of the desert. He had no desire to join his ancestors, who had fled from Egypt only to be buried as tokens of Moses' jealous deity, a vanquished people who functioned as an object lesson about what comes of questioning the omnipotence of the only God. He took the goatskin from Rachel. "Be careful with the water. I don't know how long it will be before we come across a well."

Lazarus glanced behind him. Two men on camels rode toward him. They were followed by a rotund man astride a donkey. Lazarus adjusted his leather mask. The camel riders wore the raven-coloured robes of Bedouin. The man on the donkey was dressed in a pied-coloured wool coat and breeches. Tethered behind the fat man's mount was a smaller donkey laden with bundles.

The Bedouin struck the front legs of their camels with long, thin sticks. The camels spit and gnashed their teeth. They folded their legs under them, allowing their riders to dismount with ease. The taller of the two Bedouin helped the fat man off his donkey. The other Bedouin, on seeing the women, pulled up a scarf from around his neck, concealing the holes where his nose and lips had once been.

The tall Bedouin bowed, touching his forehead and both sides of his chest with his fingertips. "Salaam."

"And peace be with you." Lazarus held his arms out to his sides to show he wore no weapons.

"Please excuse my brother, Kalil, but he has lost the power of speech," the man said, dipping his head at the scarfed Bedouin, who hid behind his camel.

The donkey man waddled over to Sarah and Rachel. His thighs trembled with each step he took. He hiked up the waistband of his breeches over his immense belly. "Shalom to you too," he said, leering at Rachel, then pointed at Sarah. "This one must be at least a hundred." He touched Rachel's sunburnt cheek. "Cover up when you're out here or you'll look like her."

The tall Bedouin frowned. "Again I must excuse a rudeness. Though my brother has no tongue he has manners, unlike my companion, who has a voice but no courtesy behind it."

"Hajid, watch it, don't forget who's paying you." The short man huffed as he walked over to Lazarus. "Speaking of insults, who shit on your face?"

Lazarus maintained his silence. He kept his eyes trained on the scimitar slipped through the belt of Hajid's robe. The Bedouin went to his camel, removed a large water bag, and drank from it.

The obese little man winked at Rachel. "Come with me; I'll see to it that you wear only silk."

61

"Don't bother her. She belongs to him," Sarah squawked.

"And just who is he that I should care?"

"He's Lazarus."

"I still don't know why I should care who he is."

"Haven't you heard the story of Lazarus, the man who was brought back from the dead?" Sarah asked.

Rachel startled the strangers when she wailed, "Beware, beware. For thine own judgement is at hand. Blessed be those who see and know the power of the Almighty. Shed no tears for those who see but do not believe, for their inheritance is everlasting torment."

The man waved her away. "Forget it. You can keep her."

Kalil pulled at Hajid's sleeve. He made signs with his hands as he moved his mouth to form painful, incoherent sentences.

Hajid nodded. "Aaron, what the old woman tells you is true. Kalil has heard stories about such a man from other travellers."

"And just who worked this miracle?"

"Our Lord and Saviour, Jeshua," Rachel sang out.

Aaron's fat belly escaped his breeches. "Would this be the same Jeshua ben Joseph who has been running around preaching about loving your neighbour and turning the other cheek?"

"You have seen our Lord?" Rachel asked.

Aaron rubbed the side of his face. "I've had the pleasure." The sting of Jeshua's hand came back to him. Aaron's remembrance of how an otherwise beautiful day in Jerusalem was spoiled when Jeshua arrived with his crew of disciples brought the taste of bile to his throat. On seeing the various tradesmen and money changers engaged in commerce on the steps of the Temple, Jeshua went insane. He kicked over tables, scattered money, and destroyed the merchants' goods. His followers, taking their master's lead, chased the businessmen away from the Temple. Aaron forced a smile. "One day I hope to have the chance to repay him. Good merchants never forget a debt."

"Neither do I," Lazarus said, walking over to a camel to pat it on its snout.

The beast rolled its head and sank its teeth into Lazarus' arm. Kalil smashed his fist into the side of the camel's jaw and yanked Lazarus free. The bite mark on Lazarus' arm was so deep that the bone was exposed. Within a few minutes, the bloody wound disappeared.

Hajid shoved Kalil away from Lazarus. He clutched Lazarus by his wrist, pulled the arm under his nose, hunting for some trace of the wound. "Truly it is a sign from God."

Aaron whistled in disbelief. "It's a sign all right, a sign that we have stumbled across a gold mine." He snapped his fingers at Kalil. "Break out some refreshments. We have business to transact." The mute unfurled a straw mat on the sand and placed dried fruit, bread, cheese, and a clay vessel of wine on top of it. "Sit, my friend. We have things to talk about."

"Tend to my mother first," Lazarus said.

Kalil removed the food and drink from the straw mat. He brought it over to the bush, resetting it in front of Sarah. He poured a good measure of date wine into a goblet fashioned out of a gourd. She drank greedily from the cup.

"Rachel, have some of this, it's delicious."

"There is no wine sweeter than the words of our Lord, no bread more nourishing than His teachings."

Aaron's immense stomach undulated under his coat. He chuckled, sounding like a boar digesting a meal. "Love, I don't think we are talking about the same man."

"That is because my Teacher is more than just a common man. He is all that Isaiah promised and more."

"Listen, darling, the Jeshua I know has managed to surround himself with whores for his pleasure, thieves to fill his coffer, and poor ignorant fishermen and farmers to do his bidding."

Rachel stretched out her hands like talons. She landed knees first on the fat man's belly. "Get her off me before she claws my eyes out," Aaron squealed. The Bedouin were convulsed with laughter.

Lazarus lifted Rachel by the back of her robe. He carried her over to Sarah. "Sit there until we've finished conducting business." He picked up the jug of wine, took one long draw out of its spout and handed it to Rachel. "Drink some of this. It will calm you down."

Rachel looked at Sarah who had somehow managed to fall asleep during all the commotion. She took the empty goblet from the old woman, filled it and gave the wine jug back to her husband.

Lazarus returned to the trader, who was sitting on his backside with his legs pointing out in front of him. He offered him the jug. "No, thank you," Aaron panted while he tried to regain his composure. "Is she always like this?"

"Like what?"

"You know, so, so…" Aaron stumbled for a discreet way of saying what was on his mind.

Hajid broke in, "So devoted. It is seldom that one gets a chance to meet a true believer."

"Five more minutes and she would have made a convert out of me." Aaron rubbed a knot on the back of his head. "Take a look at her, that bit of exercise must have exhausted the poor thing." Rachel had fallen asleep, draping her body over Sarah's. "Oh well, they deserve a little rest. Let's talk business until they come to."

"Go slowly," Lazarus said. " I have never been very good at that sort of thing."

"Don't concern yourself. Leave the details to me. Have another drink."

Lazarus took one more long draw of the wine. "It's very sweet."

"Sweeter to some than others, eh, Hajid?" The Bedouin smiled and told his brother to gather up the straw mat and food.

"Shush, be careful not to wake them," Aaron said, motioning Lazarus to take another drink.

"Come on, finish it off," Aaron cajoled. He quickly moved to sell his proposal to Lazarus. He informed Lazarus that he wanted to put him on display and charge people to look at him. "There is a fortune to be made out of our partnership."

Lazarus drained the rest of the jug's contents. "Forget it."

"It will be done tastefully," the trader assured him.

"No!" Lazarus' lips tingled, his vision blurred. He felt his feet grow numb. "I am not some freak to be paraded in front of the curious." His ears began to ring. His legs melted underneath him as he toppled backward.

Aaron's immense face appeared above Lazarus, blocking out his view of the sun. "We could both do very well by this venture."

Lazarus struggled to his feet, fighting to emerge from the stupor of the drugged wine.

"It'll be a family affair. I'll find a way of working your mother and wife into the performance." The trader's voice seemed to be coming from the bottom of a deep pit.

"Leave my family out of this!" Lazarus swung his arms at the nebulous forms of the three men drifting in and out of his sight.

"There's no reasoning with him. Get some rope and tie him up," Aaron said. "One way or another he'll join us."

Lazarus pulled his arms apart, breaking the stiff length of cord that Kalil had wrapped around his wrists.

"Your brother can't do anything right." Aaron's multi-tiered chins flapped against his neck as Hajid brought an iron bar smashing down on Lazarus' head.

"Get something stronger to hold him. Maybe by the time we get to Revivim we can convince him to see things our way."

"What about the women?" Hajid asked.

"We'll display them alongside him as the sorceresses who summoned this demon from Sheol."

"We are tempting fate. If her God is powerful enough to bring a man back from the grave, think how much easier it will be for him to send us to it." Hajid looked over at Kalil, who had emitted an animal-like shriek to gain their attention. The mute's hand came to rest on the hilt of his sword. He pulled down the scarf, stretching the orifice that functioned as a mouth across his face. He slashed his finger across his throat.

"Even my brother is worried. He thinks it's better to leave them alone and get out of here, before they recover and call down the vengeance of their God upon us."

"Be calm. With a little gentle persuasion they'll come around our way."

The Bedouin placed his hand behind Lazarus' head. He quickly pulled it back covered with blood. "He's hurt."

"He'll heal." Aaron went over to his pack donkey, opened up a bag and took out several yards of lustrous cloth. He held it away from his body by its corners. The sun's rays sparkled on the nearly transparent fabric. "Strip off the young one's clothes. Wrap this piece of silk I got in Alexandria around her."

Aaron stood above Hajid as he undid Rachel's robe. He licked his lips on seeing her naked torso. "Beautiful." He reached down to stroke her legs but stopped when she moaned. "Pity that such loveliness has to go to waste. Oh well, dress her, and let's get going."

"What about the old woman?"

"Find something suitable for her. We'll bill her as the genuine Witch of Endor."

Aaron lifted the sheer cloth wrapped around Rachel like a sarong with the big toe protruding from his sandal. "What a pity. No matter, when people get tired of the novelty of her husband, we'll have our night with her." Aaron forced himself between Kalil and Hajid. He stood on his tiptoes and laid his arms across their shoulders. "We better get moving if we want to make it to Revivim before nightfall, partners. We don't want to get caught out here by ourselves. The desert is full of untrustworthy people."

# 9

The closely packed quarters of Revivim's tavern and whoring district made the ancient cities of Sodom and Gomorrah seem righteous by comparison. Underneath the improvised awnings darkening the alleyways, prostitutes opened their robes, exposing their wares to travellers. Roman soldiers, hardened by years of fighting an elusive enemy, slipped under the awnings and fucked the whores in full view of their companions and other passersby.

As Hajid navigated the streets of Revivim, the stench of garbage and unwashed bodies gave way to the aroma of fruit and incense. On Aaron's instructions, he was to seek out the market square and locate a prime spot to set up their tent.

"The product doesn't mean shit if there's no bustle to justify the hustle," Aaron was fond of saying. "Do you think we Greeks are good merchants because it's in our blood? Of course not, we're top-notch because we seek out where the action is and move on as the music fades."

Even after hearing Aaron's routine a thousand times, invariably Hajid replied, "You're not Greek."

"I wear my nationality like a cloak. If it suits the occasion I put it on. When it doesn't, I change and wear whatever it takes to get into the party."

"Some things are not so easily put away, my friend."

"My prick may be called Aaron, but my head and heart are Stamos. Now get into town before the best spots are taken by people who have nothing better to show than old fruit."

The village market stood in an open square. Stalls, covered by brightly coloured canopies, shone like obscenely garish jewels as the sunlight washed over them. Every possible product that could be sold was represented in the market. In one stall freshly killed chickens and slaughtered goats dangled by lengths of cord tied around their feet, while the neighbouring stall displayed bolts of silk lined up like Caesar's Praetorian guards. In another booth, an old man hawking the "elixir of eternal youth", essence of bear testicles, held up a bottle containing a yellow liquid. After drinking from the vial, he disappeared behind a screen and re-emerged as a young satyr.

Hajid located an empty space two lots down from the old man's. A woman dressed in a leather bodice and sheer pleated skirt that reached only as far as her knees walked up to him. She was accompanied by a Nubian bodyguard who carried a staff the girth of Hajid's forearm. The Nubian held onto the end of a chain attached to a man restrained in a wooden scissors yoke. Around his neck he wore a sign on which only two words were written: "Sneak Thief".

"This site is not for rent." The woman fingered a charm in the shape of a dung beetle resting between her cleavage. "I'll make you a good price for that one," she said. The Nubian pointed his staff at a vacant lot at the furthest edge of the market.

"Sorry, I want this spot."

"Take the other site. It is further away, but it is out of the hot sun."

"What I have to display will not be spoiled by the sun."

"Ordinarily I reserve the main traffic alleys for locals, but seeing how you insist, I'll give it to you for twenty shekels a week."

"I want to rent it, not buy it."

"Agree to stay for two months and it's yours for eighteen shekels a week."

"Still too steep. If you could have rented it for eighteen it would be gone by now."

The woman threw her arms over her head. "You are taking advantage of me. Sixteen a week and that's my final offer. Done?"

"Not quite." Hajid lifted the scarab from between her breasts. He pretended to study it as he peered down the front of her bodice. "There is one more thing I want from you."

"Tread carefully, Bedouin."

"One more thing and the deal is done," Hajid said.

"What you ask for better be worth the pain."

"Toss in the thief's yoke. I think I can make use of it."

She was not amused. "It's not for sale."

"I will give it back to you before I leave."

"It has a sentimental value." Najar's answer had some truth to it. Back in her whoring days, when she was attempting to earn enough money to become her own master, she had a powerful Roman as a regular client. He liked to be secured in the device when naked. The sexual ritual consisted of tickling him under his scrotum with an ostrich feather and spanking him for soiling the front of her robe with his ejaculation. When he was granted a promotion to Procurator of Judea, he seized the market square from the town council, giving Najar control of it. Prior to leaving for Jerusalem, he left the yoke with her as a memento of his affection.

"Memories are fragile. Offer me something with more substance and it is yours."

Aaron's baritone voice could be heard even before Hajid entered the camp. "Pour more wine down him before he comes to, and for God's sake make sure the women are presentable."

Hajid tossed the yoke at Aaron's feet. In exchange for the apparatus, the Bedouin had given Najar an ivory-handled dagger he had lifted from the body of a Persian traveller, and a promise to visit her later. The trader strained to pick up the yoke but he could raise it no higher than his stomach.

"Do you think you can attach a pair of wrist shackles to a length of chain at either end of this thing?"

69

Hajid pulled at his beard as he inspected the yoke. "Kalil should be able to do it without much difficulty."

"Good, with the women chained to him, he's less likely to give us a problem."

Within an hour Kalil and Hajid had completed the task. They picked up the yoke and forced Lazarus' head and arms into the notches designed to immobilise a prisoner. The drugged wine had retained its potency. Lazarus stared vacantly at his surroundings. Hajid clapped the top of the yoke over Lazarus' neck and hooked a padlock through the hasp. Aaron shoved Sarah and Rachel toward the Bedouin. He fastened the shackles around their wrists.

"You have no one to blame for this except your son," Aaron said. "If he wasn't so obstinate we could have struck a deal which would have been beneficial for us all."

Sarah, dressed in a long black robe, her face smeared with kohl to make her look more terrible to the masses, spit curses without pause. "Filthy bastards! As there is a God, He'll make you pay for this."

Kalil shuddered when Sarah raised her arms and rattled her chains at him. "I swear that all your children will be born with the faces of dogs and that on your death they will devour you."

"Well played, but I suggest you save your histrionics for paying customers." Aaron lumbered over to Rachel. He pulled down the left side of her sarong. "Let's not disappoint the audience. These crowds get surly if they feel they are being cheated. So, if you don't want your husband to feel the end of a lash you had better dance when I say dance, and shake your ass when I say shake it."

Lazarus sprang to life. He aimed a kick at the trader. Aaron moved out of the way with surprising agility. "Struggle all you want. Even Samson with all his hair couldn't break out of that thing. If the Romans know how to do anything well, it's designing toys to keep their charges in line." He dropped a sack with eye holes cut in it over Lazarus' head. Part of the attraction for the spectators would be the thrill of imagining what hideous creature existed beneath the hood.

Aaron paraded his troop through the village, deliberately weaving through both the respectable and unsavoury sections of town to maximise his draw for the performance.

"See the demon brought back from the grave by the genuine Witch of Endor, servant of the evil one, advisor to King Saul. Witness the dance of death by the demon's lover."

The charlatan leaned into the face of a little girl holding the sleeve of her mother's robe. "Don't be afraid, child, these chains are magic. As long as they wear them they are in my command." Aaron cracked his whip over Rachel's head. "Dance, Jezebel."

"Stick your thumb up your ass!" Sarah jumped the length of her chain to rip his face.

Aaron reversed the handle of the whip. Wielding it like a club, he swung at Sarah but stopped, redirecting his blow at the sky. "Dance, or I'll send this useless piece of shit and her son to hell where they belong," he shouted at Rachel. A low rumble went through the minuscule group of people who had clustered around them.

Rachel closed her eyes as she gyrated her pelvis, thrusting it back and forth as if making love to an invisible suitor. "His kingdom come. His will be done. I humble myself before Him, for in His words shall I find peace and true freedom," she prayed.

# 10

Hajid pressed his lips to Najar's naked breasts. She slid her body up until his face was inside her open thighs.

"This is where you belong."

Hajid arched his back. "Aaron is expecting me."

"Once again you will be the only audience he has."

Her words were humiliating, but true. Aaron's feeble attempt to draw a crowd was a failure. The first three days a dozen people came to see him pace in front of a tent. At the conclusion of a speech full of hyperbole, he would move aside a curtain, exposing his shackled captives. Over the next two months, the audience went from sparse to almost non-existent. If it were not for the few faithful horny men who came to ogle Rachel, Aaron would have had no spectators at all. People quickly grew bored of listening to the old woman spew out her insults. Rachel's prophecies, delivered virtually in the nude, grew tedious. And as for Lazarus, his stone-like countenance and muteness provided about as much excitement as watching the rain wash away a pile of dung. Even the hawker of bear piss drew twice as many people.

When Hajid arrived, Aaron was sitting in front of his tent digging a trench in the dirt with the point of his knife. "If I don't come up with something soon, we'll all starve."

"We should let them go and return to doing what we know best," Hajid said.

"I can tell from the stench of that whore's perfume what you do best." Aaron recanted when the Bedouin clutched the handle of his scimitar. "Don't get upset. I know you're only sleeping with her to keep her off our backs about the rent."

"Kalil says we brought a curse upon ourselves."

"The only curse we've been a party to is the curse of our own stupidity. Hundreds of strangers pass through this village every day, yet we seem unable to find a way of enticing them to come here. Romans, Syrians, Greeks, I ask you, what is the one thing they all have in common?"

Hajid hated it when Aaron insisted on playing riddles instead of getting to the point. "They are all foreigners."

"No, what separates them from these Jewish peasants is that they don't want an exhibition." Aaron placed his hand on Hajid's shoulder. "They demand a spectacle."

Hajid stood outside the gates of the wall enclosing Revivim. Fashioned out of native stone and mud, the wall had been constructed by the Canaanites to protect themselves against the marauding hordes who descended on their land from the East. Led by Joshua, the nomads spared no living creature who stood to challenge their people's claim to the land. Later, when the tribes of Israel secured title to the land, they too became victims of conquest. Unlike the Canaanites, the people of Moses endured. They endured even when Babylonia laid waste the temple, enslaving God's "chosen people". From this point onward, Israel enjoyed only brief moments of independence separated by centuries of subjection to foreigners who humiliated it before the very tabernacle of its ineffable deity.

A young officer of Rome sandwiched between two grizzled veterans walked through the gates of Revivim. Hajid called out to them. "Brothers, where are you off to?"

The officer stepped from between his two companions and looked Hajid up and down. Lysias respected the Bedouin. Unlike the Zealots, the Bedouin met their enemies face to face, relying on courage and martial skills to defeat their foes.

A tall, sour-faced Jew carrying a bundle of sticks on his back inched his way toward Hajid and the soldiers. He approached close

73

enough to hear what was being said by Hajid, maintaining enough distance to avoid drawing attention to himself.

"Although I am no seer, friends, I sense you are in search of a light caress, the sweet perfume of one of our flowers of the desert."

A scowling grey-bearded soldier jabbed his finger into Hajid's chest. "We don't need the help of a poet to find what we're looking for. We're not after love; all we want is a warm tart for a couple of hours."

Hajid batted away the soldier's hand. "If that's all you desire, why not go back to your camp and sneak up on some unsuspecting horse? Its ass is just as warm, just as tight, and, from the looks of you, smells better than what you're accustomed to bedding down with."

The soldier reached for the sword tucked through his girdle.

"I didn't mean to offend to you, sir." Hajid swallowed his pride.

"Maybe you didn't mean to, but you did." Before Titus could pull out his sword, Lysias slung him into the arms of the other soldier.

"You're in my charge. I decide when we fight. And right now I think it's more profitable to fuck." Lysias turned to Hajid. "What are you selling?"

"Selling? I am not selling anything. I am giving you a chance to witness one of our humble country's true marvels, a man summoned back from the grave by two of the most awesome conjurers the world has ever known: one a witch so hideous and malevolent that the mere waft of her breath is enough to curdle milk; the other a beauty, a vision of sensuality who possesses the power to restore the dead to life to do her bidding."

Lysias moved within a nose length of Hajid. "What is the name of this fellow brought back from the grave?"

"Name, General? Since when do demons have names? He could be called Lazarus for all I know or care."

The bale of sticks strapped across the beggar's back fell to the ground. The beggar scooped up his bundle with a nimbleness that Lysias had not seen in any of the mendicants he had run across in his travels. He was about to order his men to seize the Jew when Hajid blew a kiss across his palm.

"Ah, general, you should see the demon's lover. Her beauty is unsurpassed. Imagine a woman so exquisite that death opens its gates for her."

"I'm a lieutenant." Lysias looked around. The beggar had disappeared. "Did either of you see where that Jew standing behind us went?"

"Since when do I care where a stinking Jew goes?" Titus answered.

"He didn't move like a peasant," Lysias observed.

"Ever since we killed that bunch near the garrison at Masada, you've been as jumpy as a cat."

"They were trying to surrender."

"So what? They would have ended up dying in the copper mines or on a galley."

"Three of them escaped. Three of them who can run back to their camp and spread the word of our treachery."

"Tell me the bastards didn't deserve to die. You've seen the bodies of our men rotting on the desert, stripped naked, their balls cut off and stuffed into their mouths. My only regret is, I didn't get a chance to butcher their women and children."

"Will you knock it off? This Bedouin has sparked my interest." Antonio was tired of watching Titus play the part of the angry veteran to Lysias' concerned commander.

Titus pointed at Hajid. "It better be all you say it is or I'll wear your ears on my belt."

"I promise, you will not be disappointed," Hajid responded.

As they marched through Revivim, Titus called out to other soldiers to join them. Soon a small phalanx of Romans fell into parade formation behind them. The procession attracted the attention of the inhabitants of the village and its transients. The civilians followed the soldiers to the village market.

Concealed in the crowd was the tall Jew, his back hunched to make him look shorter. When the crowd entered the market square,

Bartholomew slipped away and hid behind an empty stall. He removed the bundle of sticks from his back, leaned them against the wall and untied the cord holding them together. The faggots separated. A Roman battle sword fell to the earth. Its short blade, designed to be used in close-quarter combat, had been tempered with the blood of his fellow Jews before he removed it from a soldier he had stalked in the narrow alleyways of Jerusalem. While the soldier writhed on the ground, his hands pressed against the gushing wound across his throat, Bartholomew plunged the pagan's own sword through his heart. He prayed that the blood of a thousand more Romans and traitors would sanctify its blade in the months to come.

Burning torches surrounded Aaron's tent. Outside the circle of flames the world was dark. Titus and Antonio muscled through the people to the head of the gathering. The tinkling of bells and the beating of a drum commenced. The crowd pressed forward. Hajid ignited a pot of sulphur and camphor with a torch. Through the cloud of yellow smoke Kalil appeared, shaking and beating a timbrel. Kalil's black robe was decorated with luminous symbols of the zodiac. His face was hidden behind a horned featureless mask. He gave the skin of the timbrel a resounding thump. Hajid touched off the powder of another smudge pot. Aaron leapt through the door of the tent.

"Stand back!" Aaron intoned in his most solemn voice, "This one failed to heed my warning." He snatched the mask off Kalil. The mutilated face of the Bedouin was made even more hideous by the red henna traced around his mouth and the green paint circling his eye sockets. The crowd howled at a trick well executed.

"If you suffer from fainting spells, if your heart is weak, leave now." When Kalil struck the timbrel, Aaron flung open the tent flap. Lazarus faced the crowd, his arms and neck fastened in the yoke. His body, covered only in a loin cloth, had been painted white. The same designs appearing on Kalil's robe had been drawn on his torso. At Lazarus' feet, kneeling as if in supplication, were Sarah and Rachel.

"Don't shed tears for these women. They are the confidants and servants of Baal." Aaron cracked his whip and Hajid stepped forward.

He jerked Sarah to her feet. She had been stripped naked, dyed yellow and splashed with green blotches.

The whip cracked again. Hajid pushed Rachel toward the front of the gathering. Her naked body glistened from olive oil coating every inch of skin. Encircling Rachel's forehead was a gold band with a single blue paste jewel suspended from its centre. Tied around her waist was a long sash made from the silk sarong.

Aaron poked Sarah with the handle of his whip. "Suckled on the poison contained within those breasts, the beast gained strength."

Sarah lifted her head and spit at Aaron. "Don't listen to him. He's a liar and a thief."

"See how the witch tries to cast her spell, even though she knows as long as she and her daughter are chained to the beast her power is gone." Aaron dragged Rachel into the circle of light provided by the torches. "Dance, bitch."

Titus stared hungrily at Rachel, elbowing Antonio in his ribs. "Now there's something worth coming to see."

"Just to see?"

"Trust me, before the night is over I'll do more than look."

"Don't count on it. As long as Lysias is with us, the most we'll get tonight is a case of lice from the whores in the village."

Aaron whirled around, laying the lash across Lazarus' chest. "I said dance." Rachel slowly began to rotate her hips. She stretched out her arms to the side, moving her stomach up and down. Her voice rose in prayer but her words were drowned out by the methodical beat of Kalil's timbrel.

"This one, using her body to satiate the carnal desires of the beast, draws his evil power into herself." Aaron pulled Rachel's sash and spun her around like a top. She landed at Lazarus' feet. "But how, you ask, did this humble peddler come to master the beast and his hand-maidens?"

"No one asked, you fool. Get the girl to dance some more," Titus yelled.

"In good time, in good time," Aaron responded cautiously. Once, in Tiberius, he had spoken too harshly and nearly lost his tongue to a drunken soldier. He picked up a torch and extended the flame toward Lazarus. "When travelling through the land of the Dead Sea, a place so barren, so cursed that even the Gods disowned it, I slipped into a cave to escape the oppressive heat. While resting, I heard unholy laughter coming from a passage. I felt my way through the hellish cavern along a wall rippling with vermin and found myself looking down a precipice at this beauty." Aaron tipped the torch so its light fell on Rachel. "She was kneeling on all fours while the beast mounted her like a stallion, ramming his member in and out of her."

"Sodomite," someone called out from the crowd.

Titus winked at Antonio. "Bet Lysias would've liked to have been on the receiving end of that action."

Hajid hauled Sarah over to Aaron. "Seated on a throne built from the pelvis and leg bones of some ancient race of giants, this sorceress goaded the demon on, exhorting him to push harder, further into the orifice of his concubine. I watched in horror as the demon and his lover performed one unnatural act after another, afraid to move or breathe lest they hear me and exact a horrible revenge. After two days of nonstop intercourse, they collapsed, exhausted."

Looking up at the heavens Aaron clasped his hands together. "It is said that if a righteous man can chain the hands of a demon when he is sleeping then that creature must obey the will of that man. I crept up on the fiend while he slept and snared the beast in his own lair, taking his concubine and mother hostage." Aaron lowered his head, retreated from the crowd, awaiting its reaction. He knew that the story needed more work, but that would come with time and practice.

"Do you expect us to believe this pathetic freak is one of Aazel's devils?" a man at the rear of the crowd hollered.

"Of course not. My honest story is just that, a story, until you see the proof of my words." Regardless of how poorly Aaron had related the tale up until this point, his finale would leave the crowd speechless.

Kalil beat his timbrel, joined by Hajid piping a shrill melody on a shepherd's flute.

"Evil cannot die."

Hajid ceased playing and drew his scimitar from its scabbard. He sliced the head of one the torches from its shaft and laid the sword in Aaron's outstretched hands.

Aaron backed up until he felt Lazarus' breath on his neck. He raised the sword saying, "Evil cannot die." The blade swept diagonally across Lazarus' chest. Blood spurted onto the crowd. Aaron cut a gash in the other direction, leaving a bloody X on the stonecutter's naked torso. He rubbed a mixture of salt and charcoal ash into the wound. Lazarus strained against the yoke. A slight cracking of the wood went undetected.

"Heal thyself, demon." Aaron stood back so the gathering could see the bloody X disappear. To further satisfy their curiosity, he soaked a cloth in vinegar and cleaned the area surrounding the wound. Not a trace of a scar remained.

"Evil cannot die," Aaron repeated in a hushed, reverent tone. "It can only be controlled." He entered the tent, lowering the flap behind him. Kalil and Hajid dragged Rachel into the tent after Aaron. They left Sarah tied to a post outside to bear the jeers and insults of the crowd.

Prompted by the Romans' shouts of "Bravo!" the people stamped their feet until Aaron came out with Hajid and Kalil. Raising his arms, Aaron bowed graciously. The Bedouin circulated through the audience with small brass pots. Aaron's face flushed every time he heard the clink of coins. He receded into the tent rubbing his hands together.

When the crowd had thinned out, Titus held up a gold coin with the likeness of the Emperor Tiberius stamped on its surface. Kalil waited for the Roman to drop the coin into his pot. Titus lifted his other hand. A piece of silver was pinched between his thumb and finger. "This one is for the show. The other is for a private session for my friend and me."

Kalil shook his head as he moved away from the Roman. Titus grabbed the Bedouin by his arm and flipped him to the ground. Hajid dashed over and stepped on his brother's hand, preventing him from slipping it under his robe and pulling out a knife.

Hajid placed himself between Kalil and Titus. "What's the problem, sir? Didn't you like the show?"

"Liked it, I loved it. That's what I was telling this idiot." Titus dropped the silver coin into Hajid's pot. "I got a gold eagle here for your master if he lets me into the tent to get a close up view of the demon's lover."

"He's my partner, not my master." Hajid said. "How close a view do you want?"

"For what I need to see this is about right." Titus held up his index fingers and measured off about eight inches.

"Boy do you have delusions of grandeur, a thumb's length and a straw's width is the real measure," Antonio joked.

"What I have to offer is three times more meat than that whore has ever received from anyone or anything."

"That's enough," Lysias commanded. "We've come here to relax. There are plenty of women in town."

"But this is the one I want." Titus shoved Hajid out the way and entered the tent.

Aaron was on his knees in front of his money box. He slammed the lid shut. "The next show's tomorrow evening."

Titus leered at Rachel sitting in the corner with her knees drawn up to her chest to hide her nakedness. He held the gold coin up to an oil lamp suspended from the cross-brace of the tent. The light danced across the polished surface of the coin.

Aaron struggled to his feet. "Of course, sir. But I must warn you this one has evil powers that…"

Titus glared, closed his fist around the coin. "Shut up and leave." Aaron bobbed his head up and down, picking up the money box on his way out. As he backpedalled he bumped into Antonio and Lysias.

Lazarus, imprisoned beyond the light of the lamp, lifted his head. A voice from a place beyond the grave filled the tent with the musty smell of a tomb. "Touch her and I'll kill you."

Titus swung the lamp toward the back of the tent. "So the demon speaks. After I get through with your darling, I'll see if you can scream."

Lysias placed his hand on Titus' forearm. "I told you that we didn't come here for this. There are plenty of women in town."

"But this is the one I want."

"I didn't want to resort to this, but you have left me no choice. Antonio, I order you to arrest Centurion Titus for insubordination."

"You what!" Titus pivoted on one heel and slammed his forearm into Lysias' nose. The lieutenant crumpled to the ground, dazed, his legs spread out in front of him.

"When you have fought as many battles as I have, seen as many Romans butchered as I have, then maybe you'll earn the right to order me." Titus planted his foot against Lysias' chest, pushing him flat on his back. "Hold him while I entertain myself, Antonio. I'll give you a go at her when I'm finished."

"This is mutiny," Lysias croaked, and tried to get up. Antonio pressed a knee on his lieutenant's throat.

Rachel crawled to Lazarus. "Fear not, for the Lord is my Shepherd. I commend myself to Him. His will be done."

Titus backhanded Rachel full force. "Commend yourself to me. I'm the one who holds your fate in my hands."

He unfastened his leather girdle. His pleated skirt fell around his ankles, exposing a shrivelled penis. Titus forced Rachel's face toward his waist, but stopped when he heard a screech. He turned to see Antonio lift his arms over his head as a sword pushed through his back and out the front of his stomach. Titus stared at Bartholomew. The Jew had impaled his comrade like a shrike skewering an insect on a thorn. Titus grabbed his belt and rolled across the ground to his feet. Both his hands were wrapped around the hilt of his sword. He lunged, but tripped over the skirt bunched around his ankles.

81

As Titus got up, the thunderous crack of the yoke splitting in half diverted his attention from Bartholomew. Lazarus roared and sprang forward, swinging one end of the broken yoke. The first blow dislocated the Roman's jaw. The second blow cleaved his face from the top of his nose to his upper lip. Titus tottered on the edge of consciousness, feebly slashing at an enemy he could hear but no longer see through the blood filling his eyes.

Bartholomew kicked the legs out from under the Roman. Weaving his fingers through Titus' hair, he slit his throat and pitched him face down next to Lysias. The young lieutenant moaned. Bartholomew wrapped his hands around the pommel of his sword. He raised the weapon, aiming the tip of its blade at Lysias' heart.

"No, don't kill him! He tried to stop them," Lazarus cried out.

"As you wish," Bartholomew said. He wiped his sword clean on Titus' skirt and tossed the garment over Lysias' face. "Come into the light." He touched the stonecutter's grey, scaly flesh. "Is there anything good that comes out of Nazareth?" he asked.

Lazarus searched for clothing for himself and the women. By the time he left the tent, Aaron and the Bedouin had disappeared. The commotion had convinced them that it was time to find another location to exercise their profession.

"We better get out of here before those Romans are missed," Bartholomew said.

When they had safely passed through the gates of Revivim, Bartholomew glanced at the sky. "Good, the moon's out so we can travel at night and put some distance between the soldiers and us."

"You think the Romans will follow us?" Lazarus asked.

"If not them, Herod's lackeys."

Bartholomew's eyes wandered over the hilly terrain, finally resting on a massive wedge-shaped boulder. "That's where I first ran across Jeshua. He'd gone up there to fast for forty days. If it hadn't been for me, more than likely he would have starved."

Lazarus felt his throat constrict. "So you're a follower of Jeshua."

"I haven't decided yet. I'm waiting for a sign." Bartholomew started climbing the hill. "We'll camp there. It'll be a good spot for the women to recuperate."

When they reached the top of the hill, Bartholomew surveyed the land below. From this vantage point, he would be able to see if anyone had managed to track them. A ledge protruding from the other side of the boulder blocked the sun. It cast a cooling shadow over the women as they settled down to sleep.

Bartholomew searched through his rucksack and took out a sharpening stone. He placed his sword across his lap. "Judas and Simon told me about you. They said if I doubted the power of Jeshua I should find you." He spit on the whetstone, rubbing his saliva into it with his thumb, and skimmed it down the blade. "So I did. That Roman pig and his friend were an unexpected bonus."

Lazarus took the sword and the stone away from Bartholomew. He quickly honed the blade to the keenness of a razor. "The trick is to let the stone do the work," Lazarus said.

Bartholomew licked his thumb and tested the blade's edge. "I'm trying to find someone, something to believe in," he said. "I thought Jeshua might be the one our people have been waiting for."

"Is he?"

"The first time I ran across him he seemed to have something that separated him from other men. Now, I'm not sure."

"He is the light and the way." Rachel rose from her nap and threw a pebble at Lazarus. "Who are we to question the ways of the Anointed One?"

Bartholomew grinned at Rachel. "I don't know what it is with Jeshua, but he attracts women to him like bees to nectar."

"Or flies to shit," Lazarus responded.

Rachel glided toward them. "Oh, you of little faith. We are like the blades of grass compared to Him. We are like the flowers on the blades of grass who will wither and die without Him."

"She's good. I ought to introduce her to Matthew. He's always breaking his head to come up with some saying, some parable, that he can attribute to Jeshua." Bartholomew slung his pack over his shoulder and started to walk away. "When the sun goes down, head over the knoll; keep to the hills."

"Where are you going?"

"Capernaum."

"Aren't you afraid you'll be captured?"

Bartholomew laughed. "The only face that lieutenant saw was yours."

"But I saved his life."

"Think about it. You left a Roman officer alive in the same tent as the bodies of his men. You left him to account for why he survived and explain why he didn't suffer so much as a scratch."

"So now I'm wanted by the Romans."

Bartholomew shrugged as if to say there are worse things. "You should be safe. The Romans will be expecting you to go north. They can't imagine anyone fleeing toward the Dead Sea."

Rachel rushed Bartholomew and held onto his sleeve. "Look at this man, risen from the grave by the word of the living God. Go tell the people. This is your sign!"

Sarah's voice surfaced from beneath the ledge. "Girl, he's not a sign. He's a question in search of an answer."

# 11

To pass the time as they walked, Sarah spoke of the mountains to the north rising out of Lebanon. She recounted stories she had heard of vast tracts of cedar growing next to snow-fed streams that flowed from the mountains to the desert, where each drop of moisture was sopped up by the thirsty land.

Lazarus felt oddly at peace in the harsh surroundings. Each step he took awakened sensations left dormant since his resurrection. His eyes wandered over the Valley of the Great Rift, barren with the exception of an occasional wild flower or stubborn shrub that had forced its way through cracks in the sandstone and dolomite rock formations that created the ridges bordering the valley. He looked up. The sky was white with flocks of sea-gulls sailing on the air currents. He knew the presence of the gulls meant Yam ha-Melah, the great basin of the Dead Sea, was nearby.

Sarah valiantly pushed herself through the heat, making small talk to maintain her connection with her son. "Your grandmother, Hashem bless her, told me that Yam ha-Melah was poisoned when Lot tossed his wife's body into its waters." She wiped off the sweat trickling down her cheek, licking her own moisture from her palm. "Lot slept with his daughters."

"They got him drunk first," Lazarus responded.

Sarah mumbled, "That's how the story finally came to us, but I don't believe it."

Rachel was oblivious to the heat. She scrambled ahead of Lazarus. Upon reaching higher ground she spread out her arms, looked at the landscape below, and praised Hashem for creating such a magnificent world. "It's beautiful. You can see the holy city."

Two dozen squat white buildings comprising the compound of Qumran sat atop a single column of stone which stood like a sentry among the lesser rocks. Mist from the Dead Sea rose above the desert as the approaching night cooled its waters. Before the sun set, the enclave of religious fanatics and mystics would vanish as the fog spiralled upwards.

"Truly, it is the New Jerusalem. Come up here, Mother Sarah," Rachel exclaimed. The old woman began the arduous climb toward her daughter-in-law, knowing that Rachel would give her no peace until she joined her.

"Lazarus!" A scream shattered the tranquillity of the wilderness. Lazarus jerked his head in their direction. His eyes followed his wife's terrified gaze. He froze when he saw his mother thrashing her arms as she executed a frenzied dance over a patch of smooth pebbles. Sarah's effort to maintain her balance was fruitless. With an expression of resignation she fell, tumbling down the steep embankment.

"Mother, Mother, are you all right?" Lazarus' hands travelled over her arms and legs searching for broken bones.

The old woman struggled to raise one hand in the air. Her voice, though stitched with pain, was clear. "Don't ask stupid questions."

"We'll go back to Revivim. We'll find someone there to help you." Lazarus slipped his arms under the old woman's body and started to lift her.

"Don't touch me!" Sarah coughed blood and called out to Rachel.

Rachel sprinted down the hill and knelt beside the old woman. "Yes, Mother."

"It hurts."

"Be still, nothing is going to happen to you. You'll get better," Lazarus said.

"She can't get any better than she already is. She has seen the Master; the kingdom of heaven is hers. She is a believer."

"A believer?" Sarah patted Rachel's hand. "Sing for me."

Rachel sang a longing note of praise to the Son of Man made God. "I'm cold."

"We'll make camp here until you get better." Lazarus raced off to comb the hills for bits of dried brush and twigs.

Sarah turned her face toward Rachel. "Your man needs you."

Rachel wrapped her arms around herself and stuck out her bottom lip. "He's not my man. He doesn't belong to me and he most certainly doesn't claim the right of ownership over me. I am a slave to only one being and His kingdom is not of this world."

"If only I had the strength, I'd give you such a slap." Sarah waved a frail outstretched hand. Even this insignificant gesture tortured the old woman. "You think this journey is all about your Rabbi?"

"Of course it is. Everything that has happened has been to fulfil the Teacher's destiny."

"So our being paraded around back in Revivim was part of some grand plan?" Each word coming from Sarah gave birth to a furrow of agony around her mouth.

Rachel thought a moment. "I think we were being tested to see if we were worthy."

"Enough! Worthiness has nothing to do with the hell we've been put through."

Rachel flipped her head and glared at the old woman. "Go on."

Sarah clicked her tongue against the roof of her mouth. "Without my son, your Messiah is just another one of the fanatics who wander out of the desert to face ridicule."

"He is the Messiah. His words are the truth."

"That may be." A searing flame coursed through Sarah's body. "Lazarus is because he has to be. Jeshua is because Lazarus is."

"You're confusing me."

"Stop it! Use your wits to serve yourself and your husband."

"My calling is to serve the Chosen One. "

Sarah squeezed her eyelids shut. If she did not look at her crippled body, perhaps the pain would go away. She was wrong. Every time she inhaled, her rib cage crushed her heart and lungs.

It was after dusk when Lazarus returned with his arms laden with whatever fuel he was able to find. He gathered a few stones, forming a circle out of them. "There's not much around here to burn, so we'll have to make the best use of what there is."

Rachel picked up a bush, breaking off its dead branches. "You could never keep a fire going, much less start one on your own." She placed the bits of kindling inside the circle of stones and arranged a layer of brown grass over them. "Give me the flints." A spark jumped to the dried grass as she struck the two blue pieces of stone together. Puffs of smoke rose from the grass. Holding her hair back, she leaned forward, fanning the infant fire with her free hand. Within a few seconds, tongues of fire danced on top of the bed of kindling.

Sarah shifted her weight toward the fire. "Sit next to me. Warm me between your bodies."

Rachel took Lazarus' hand in hers. He looked at the small delicate fingers touching his broken, callused skin. She led him over to Sarah. They huddled together.

Rachel inhaled the odour of the burning brush and twigs. She closed her eyes, imagining she was breathing in the sweet aroma of pine and cedar. She rubbed her hand over Sarah's knee and proceeded to describe the phantom scent to her but was interrupted by the old woman.

"The brooks... Listen closely... Hear the waters from the mountains of Lebanon," Sarah prattled as she slipped into a state of delirium which mercifully numbed the body, as well as the mind. "The water sings."

"She'll get better," Rachel lied as she tucked her knees to her chest and slept.

Sarah rested her head on Lazarus' shoulder. Each rasping breath sounded as if it would be her last. Lazarus peered into the darkness, keeping his ears tuned for any sound besides the wind whistling through the hills. As the fire died, Lazarus eased the women off him. Sarah moaned. The chill of the evening rippled through her bruised body. Lazarus tossed the remainder of the sticks he had collected on the red embers. His spine stiffened when he heard a noise in the rocks behind him.

Lazarus dropped to his stomach and pressed his ear against the cold earth. The sound of more than one person's footsteps vibrated through the ground. Without success, his hands sought out something he could use as a weapon. Again he heard the noise, less obvious than the first time but more sinister because of its deliberate softness. He flattened himself on the earth, slithering on his belly through the dirt toward a clump of boulders.

Three men inched their way through the cover of rocks, guided by the glow of the fire, unaware of Lazarus crouching on the path in front of them. When they were nearly on him he ripped off his mask, attacking them like Samson in the valley of Ramathlehi. Unnerved, two of the men retreated to the security of the rocks, leaving their companion to face the beast alone. The remaining brigand thrust at Lazarus with a spear.

Lazarus threw back his head and bared his teeth, distorting his already gruesome visage. He clasped his hands together and swung his straightened arms like a war club. The man's eyes rolled into his head. The force of the blow drove his nose into his brain. He crumpled lifelessly to the ground. His two companions, cringing at the base of the rocks, abandoned their weapons and fled.

Lazarus picked up their swords, shoving one through the belt of his robe and holding the other one. No matter what he did, no matter where he went, he could not escape men with swords. He wished at that moment that he had been trained as a blacksmith. He would follow the words of the Torah and turn these blades into ploughshares.

When Lazarus re-entered the clearing, the fire was more fierce than it had been before he left to confront the intruders. The shapes of several men materialized behind the translucent spires of flames. The men were casting broken spear shafts and lengths of cloth bearing the images of the Roman war eagle into the fire. Lazarus did not budge while his eye searched for his wife and mother. Rachel was trapped in the arms of a large man. His hand covered her mouth. Sarah had been moved away from the fire and was lying on a crude litter. Lazarus' fingers tightened around the hilt of his sword.

"Don't be stupid. Put your arms behind your neck and lock your fingers together." The large man released Rachel. "Do as I say. It's too beautiful a night to spoil." The light of the fire flashed against the bandit's knife.

Four men dragged the body of the outlaw Lazarus had slain into camp. "Barabbas, he killed Amos with his bare hands." One of the men gave the bandit Lazarus' mask.

Barabbas poked the corpse with his foot. He flipped his knife over in his hand and rammed the pommel end into the stomach of the man who had spoken. "Where are Hosea and Enoch? This could not have happened if they'd been together."

The man doubled over, clutching his abdomen. "I don't know. They were gone by the time we arrived."

"I shouldn't overreact. It's a sign of poor leadership." Barabbas sighed and continued, "Go find them for me."

"Shall I bring them back?"

"There's no place with us for cowards." Barabbas looped his arm through the stonecutter's arm and piloted him away from the fire. He stood a foot taller than Lazarus.

"Do these two belong to you?" Barabbas asked.

"They are my wife and mother."

In the flickering light of the fire, a blue unhealthy scar running from Barabbas' earlobe to the corner of his mouth undulated like an immense leech. He pointed at the stone Sarah had fashioned to fill Lazarus' empty eye socket. "Nice work, mind if I see it?"

"It's stuck. It won't come out."

Barabbas handed Lazarus back his mask. "I could give it an assist."

"You could try," Lazarus responded.

"I've had my fill of that kind of sport today." Barabbas flicked a twig off Lazarus' shoulder.

Rachel crawled unnoticed over to Barabbas. She startled him when she shrilled, "The day is but an eye blink in the torment of hell that awaits those who defile the sanctity of God's messengers."

Barabbas raised his hand as if to strike her, but merely patted her head. "Talks a lot, doesn't she?" The cinch of his belt came loose; his robe fell open. His chest was latticed with the unmistakable lesions left by the lead-weighted strands of a whip. He pulled the front of his robe together and tightened his belt.

"You get used to it," Lazarus replied and walked over to Sarah.

Barabbas followed him to the litter. "What's the verdict, Elon?" The man leaning over Sarah waggled his hand. The bandit cleared his throat, spit into the fire. "Is it worth taking her with us?"

Elon shrugged. "The journey will probably kill her."

"You're pretty attached to her, aren't you?" Barabbas asked.

"She's my mother."

Barabbas ran his fingertip down the length of his scar. "See that it doesn't."

"Hear, O Israel, your judgement is at hand. He who shows mercy will yet be saved," Rachel blurted.

Barabbas cupped his hands over his ears. "For God's sake, man, can't you keep your woman quiet?"

"No."

"I don't think you'd be so quick to say that if you knew who I am."

"It would change nothing."

"You're right." The bandit crossed his legs. Without using his hands to support himself, he sat down. He slapped the ground, inviting Lazarus to join him. "I'm Barabbas, leader of this group of patriots."

Lazarus picked up a handful of dirt, closing his fist around it. The earth seeped out of the bottom of his hand while he gradually unfurled his fingers. "I've heard of you, but I don't recall ever hearing of you referred to as a patriot." Lazarus scooped up more earth. "Before I came along, mothers in my village used your name to frighten their children."

Barabbas covered his face with his huge hands and peeked from behind them. "Please, stop. You're embarrassing me. To be compared to you is an honour of which I'm not worthy."

"How do you know me?"

"It's my livelihood to know what my competitors are doing. From the look of you I'd say that Jeshua botched the job."

"Maybe, but I haven't heard of you working any wonders other than killing innocent people."

Barabbas sprang to his feet. "I find that the knife works infinitely better toward furthering our cause than all the promises of prophets and mystics exhorting us to await the coming of the Messiah." He threw his arms in front of him as though casting a net. His men stopped what they were doing and listened. Barabbas chanted in a beautiful tenor that betrayed his youthful calling as a member of the Temple chorus.

*"Thus spoke Isaiah.*
*Awake, awake.*
*Put on thy beautiful garments.*
*O Jerusalem, the holy city.*
*For henceforth there shall be no more come into thee uncircumcised and unclean. "*

He winked at Lazarus. "And you thought your wife had talent. She's got nothing on me." Barabbas extended his hand and pulled Lazarus to his feet. "I'm bringing you to my camp."

"I won't let you take us back as prisoners."

Barabbas drew his knife from its sheath, pressing its point against his scar. "I've skinned men —" he said and looked over at Rachel, "and women — with this."

Lazarus broke away from Barabbas and ran toward the fire. "I have been beyond the grave and have returned from Sheol." He directed his words at the bandit's men, trying to re-enact the routine created by Aaron. "I possess powers too horrible, too destructive for you to fathom." He thrust his hand into the midst of the flames and picked up a live coal. He closed his hand over it until he extinguished its heat in his fist.

"Well done. You've made your point." Barabbas' men whistled and applauded along with their leader. "Come with us as our guests." He waved four of his men over to where Sarah lay. They picked up the litter. Two other men formed a sling out of their arms for Rachel to sit in.

The bandits disappeared into the hills. When Barabbas was certain his men could not hear him, he said, "It's lucky for you my boys didn't smell your flesh frying or you'd find out what it's like to die a second time."

"You think I was an act?"

"I saw you pick up that fistful of dirt. You smothered the coal in it."

"You should have said something."

"It was my mitzvah."

Lazarus held out both his closed fists. He opened his left hand. In its palm was the mound of dirt. When he opened his other hand, a thin stream of smoke rose from the still red coal. He dropped it on the ground.

Barabbas reached down to touch the glowing lump, pulling back his hand when it scorched his fingertips.

# 12

The trek to Barabbas' hideout was arduous. The small band scaled cliffs littered with broken rocks and greasy slabs of slate, weaving their way single file through a narrow maze of fissures. As they passed by the pinnacle rock, where Qumran sat hundreds of feet above the desert floor, a shofar sounded.

"Damn mystics believe that by blowing that ram's horn and praying all day they'll speed up the coming of the Messiah," Barabbas grumbled.

Lazarus asked, "You don't think a Messiah will come?"

"I wouldn't miss breakfast waiting for him."

"Then why bother fighting the Romans?"

"Because they took what belongs to us."

The shofar echoed through the hills again. Barabbas covered his ears. "Bring some food up to Qumran," he ordered one of his men.

"I thought you hated them."

"Nah, I just hate their bullshit. Besides, I can't let them starve."

They continued the journey for another half-day before they halted in front of a solid wall of rock. Barabbas pushed aside a heap of tangled bushes. Behind the shrubs was a tunnel which ran so far back that it swallowed all light. Barabbas waved to the others to enter the passageway ahead of him. Following them into the tunnel, he dragged the brush behind him, concealing the opening.

After they had marched in near blackness for over an hour, a shaft of sunlight appeared. The Zealots rushed toward it. Unlike Lazarus, they found no solace in the darkness. The tunnel emptied into a boxed canyon, surrounded on all sides by walls too high and sheer for anyone to scale.

The bandit's camp — animals, people, and tents — was concealed under a huge table of rock overhanging the rim of the canyon. Women as hard and scrabbled as the cliff walls enclosing them rushed out to meet Barabbas and his men. The women were followed by a yelping pack of children and well-fed dogs. Rumour had it that the dogs were nourished on the testicles of castrated Romans. It wasn't true, but there was no harm in letting the story circulate.

A young woman with one leg hobbled toward them on a crutch made out of a forked tree limb. The bandits divided their ranks to allow her to walk through them. She pinched Rachel's upper arm. "This one's almost thin enough to be one of us," she hollered at a group women standing behind her. "Speak about being done for." She rapped the frame of the litter where Sarah lay unconscious. Lazarus stepped forward to protect his mother from the cripple's probing fingers. The woman laughed when his glare fell on her. "How long did you let this piece of meat rot in the sun?"

Barabbas raised his fist. "Esther, get away from them before I take a stick to you."

"That's no way to treat your blood."

Barabbas retreated when the women formed a protective ring around his sister.

"Take these women to my tent," Esther addressed her followers.

Elon protested. "I'm in charge of caring for the sick and wounded."

"Your idea of healing is lopping off someone's limb." She slapped at his leg with the stock of her crutch. "Now get them to my tent."

Rachel burst out in song. "When God created woman, she created the world. Blessed be the womb of woman for within it resides true strength and wisdom."

"Give it a rest, sister," Esther moaned.

"Does your wife go on like this for long?" Barabbas asked.

"Sometimes all night."

"Good," Barabbas said.

Lazarus explored the camp. Boys with the tell-tale signs of starvation, festering sores and bloated bellies, played brutal games of combat. They hacked at one another with wooden swords, whirled makeshift slings over their heads and let fly missiles that sometimes struck their friends, drawing blood along with angry shouts of pain.

Lazarus approached four men working at the far end of the camp. They were gouging three small caves out of the canyon's walls. When the holes were large enough, they hauled a bulging sack over to the deepest one and stuffed it inside. After sealing off the opening they recited Kaddish. When they were through, one of the men glared at Lazarus, maligning him to the others. "This is his doing."

Barabbas appeared behind Lazarus and growled, "Shut up and get back to work." The men hurriedly gathered up swords and spears piled to the side, placed them in the other two holes and buried them.

"Not a bad take, eh?" Barabbas' chest swelled proudly. "I have you to thank for these weapons. Seems the Romans were so determined to track down the monster who killed their men in Revivim that they stumbled right into our ambush." He slapped Lazarus on the back. "Don't be so glum. If they had caught you, the three of you would be decorating crucifixes. Now, come on. I told my slave I'd beat her if she let your food grow cold."

A group of children encircled Barabbas and Lazarus, preventing them from entering the bandit's tent. They dared each other to run up and poke Lazarus. They were undernourished replicas of their parents. Their faces were smeared with dirt; their hair was coarse and dried out. Their eyes were dull, listless, lacking spark and colour, roving constantly as if on the watch for predators.

Two older boys stabbed Lazarus in the buttocks with sharpened sticks to goad him into action. Barabbas shrugged. Lazarus hunched his shoulders, creating the illusion of a hump growing on his back, and bounded into the centre of the circle. He gnashed his teeth and roared. A small girl burst into hysterical screams.

Lazarus ended his performance. "Don't be afraid. I wouldn't hurt anyone."

"Try telling that to Amos," Barabbas said as he walked off.

The outlaw waited for Lazarus outside his tent. He held out a stick frayed at the end into whip-like tendrils. "Take this with you when you go inside. If your food is cold use it on my slave. Don't strike her in the face if you can help it."

Lazarus raised his knee and snapped the stick in half. "I've seen enough people flogged to last me two life times." He flung the pieces at Barabbas.

"Soft-hearted, eh?" Barabbas twisted his face as though he was down wind of a foul stench. "Maybe that sort of sentiment is good for your Messiah but, believe me, it doesn't cut it out here."

"He's not my Messiah!" Lazarus grabbed the bandit and shook him.

"I was wrong. You're not soft-hearted. You're soft-headed."

Lazarus released Barabbas when the shadows of several of the outlaw's men fell over them.

"It's okay, boys." Barabbas held up his hand. "A word of caution, friend." The bandit hooked his arm around Lazarus' neck and pulled him inside his tent. "Don't ever do that again. My men are very protective of me. I'm the only leader they have."

The interior of the tent was decorated with the trophies of Barabbas' expeditions. Fragile Greek vases with red and black drawings depicting the struggles of pagan heroes and gods functioned as receptacles for various lengths of lances and spears. Roman sitting pillows and meticulously hand-woven Persian carpets transformed the primitive accommodation into a space fit for a Bedouin sheik. Behind a scrim that separated the living area from the sleeping section of the tent passed the lithe silhouette of a woman.

"Cassandra, bring us something to drink."

A tall woman entered the room. Her faded white-and-blue gown was held in place at one shoulder by a brooch. Her other shoulder was bare and bore a bruise in the shape of a thumb print. Barabbas barely looked at her, consigning her to a lesser position than the other spoils of his profession. She carried a silver pitcher and two goblets on a brass tray. Her refusal to stoop and cower conveyed a nobility retained even in her servitude. She kept her eyes fixed on some invisible mark ahead of her and felt the tray for the pitcher. Barabbas guided the pitcher to his goblet. She did not move her eyes from the mark as she poured the wine.

Lazarus held out his goblet. She did not react. Her skin, burnished like polished bronze, stood in contrast to her threadbare garment. He stared into her cobalt eyes and waved a hand in front of her face. The bandit nodded. Lazarus tapped the pitcher with the rim of his goblet. She poured the wine without spilling a drop. Her blank eyes penetrated Lazarus, delving into his soul, betraying a sight she possessed that was deeper than that of the natural senses.

Lazarus avoided her gaze, attributing the intensity of her stare to her blindness. He experienced a sensation of vertigo that was not from the wine.

"Stop eyeing me."

"I can't. It is my curse."

"Your blindness?" Lazarus asked.

Her hair was tied back and fastened above her slender neck with an ivory comb. She swivelled her body like a flower searching out the rays of the sun. The waning daylight seeping through the opening of the tent touched her face. "My sight is my anathema."

As Cassandra started to leave Barabbas held her by her ankle. He reached under her gown, stroked the calf of her leg, working the length of his arm up between her thighs. She bore the intrusion of the bandit's filthy hand stoically.

"She's something else. Claims to be some kind of soothsayer. I stole her from a caravan on the way to the governor's palace in Jerusalem. The Romans love all this second sight crap."

Lazarus jerked Barabbas' arm out from under Cassandra's garment.

"You want her, eh? Can't blame you. She's a real piece of work. Too bad she's blind. She can only perform the simplest of tasks. But how much talent does she need to serve the purpose that some fat Roman intended her for?"

"Shut up and pass the wine."

Barabbas slapped Cassandra across her bottom. "Oh, you want her all right." He lifted her garment above her waist. "Have you ever seen such a perfect ass? She's the ideal mate for you, as cold and lifeless as a tomb." Cassandra wheeled around, cursing the bandit in her native tongue.

Although Barabbas did not understand her, he felt the sting of her words. "I should beat you, but I won't. I'll leave that to him." He nodded at Lazarus. "She's yours. I give her to you as a sign of our new-found friendship."

"I don't want a slave."

"Go on, take the girl and get out of here."

"I told you, I don't want a slave."

Barabbas whipped his arm to the side and knocked over a wine goblet. "I don't care what you want. She's yours. I'm sick of listening to her. All she ever does is talk about the raising of this and the destruction of that. She'll fit in just fine with that lunatic wife of yours."

Cassandra held onto a length of rope, secured at one end to a support pole inside the tent and at the other end to a lance rammed in the ground near the cooking fire. She followed the rope outside, returning with wooden bowls of lentils in each hand. Lazarus took the bowls from her, giving one to Barabbas and tossing a round of flat bread on his lap.

"You are free to go whenever you want," Lazarus said.

A faltering smile appeared on Cassandra's face. "Where would I go? The only safe course for me to pursue in this barbaric land is to remain a slave."

Lazarus felt an odd kinship with the woman. "You are free to go," he repeated.

"That is what Paris said when I told him all would be lost."

"You think your wife's got problems?" the bandit asked. "This one believes she was some sort of princess a thousand years ago in a city that was sacked by an army of Greeks."

"There are worse fates than slavery, as you will discover," Cassandra said and went out to the cooking fire.

Barabbas stretched and yawned. "She's right in her own weird way. What she has had to put up with from me is benevolent compared to what that Roman governor had in store for her. As soon as he was no longer amused by her prophecies or taken by her beauty, she would have been tossed into the soldiers' barracks."

Cassandra reappeared with a platter of pungent strips of goat meat mixed with herbs and cracked wheat. Barabbas scooped up the victuals with a piece of bread, stuffing the entire mixture into his mouth.

"Glad I gave her to you," Barabbas belched between mouthfuls. "She can't cook worth a damn." He picked up a strip of goat meat, dangling it in front of his mouth like a worm.

Finished eating, Barabbas reclined on one side and asked, "Have you thought about what you're going to do when you leave here?"

"Find Jeshua."

"Why, so he can give you back your good looks?"

"Maybe, after he gives Rachel back her mind."

"And how are you going to do all this?" Barabbas' question was met with silence. "That's what I thought. Stay with us until you decide how to get what you want from Jeshua."

"I'm not political."

"Sleep on it and we'll talk more about it in the morning."

Lazarus pointed at the dagger in Barabbas' belt. "I doubt if I could sleep with one eye open all night."

"You disappoint me. I thought you had more faith in me. After all, we are friends."

"I don't use that word as freely as you do."

"Suit yourself." Barabbas started to lead Cassandra away. Lazarus moved in front of them, barring them from entering the sleeping section of the tent.

"You gave her to me, remember?" The coldness in Lazarus' voice conveyed the intended threat.

"Fine, just make sure you two don't keep me awake all night," the bandit sneered.

"I will make our bed," Cassandra said.

Lazarus touched the soft skin of Cassandra's naked shoulder. "Find where my wife is staying; sleep there."

"Boy, can I pick them," Barabbas groaned. "She's blind. She can't go twenty feet without being attached to a rope." Barabbas stuck his head out the tent. "Elon, get in here. I know you're out there eavesdropping."

"I was waiting in case you needed me," Elon panted as he rushed into the tent.

"One day your curiosity will cost you your ears." Barabbas took Cassandra's hand and gave it to Elon. "Bring her to my sister."

# 13

For six nights in a row, Elon escorted Cassandra back and forth from Esther's tent. Lazarus rarely spoke to her except to ask how Rachel and Sarah were doing. Neither one had emerged from Esther's tent since their arrival, and since Esther had forbidden any male to enter her dwelling, Lazarus had to rely on Cassandra for news.

"They are well," she would lie. "Your woman sends her love."

"She buried her love with our children long before she buried me," Lazarus said.

When Cassandra entered Esther's tent Rachel was weaving her myth. "And He makes the lame to walk..."

Esther pounded her fist against the stump of her leg. "The lame to walk, eh?"

"And the blind to see," Rachel added.

Esther looked up at Cassandra framed in the flickering light of the oil lamp. She reached behind her back for a pillow. "Join us, Princess. Rachel is telling me all about her Messiah. He's a genuine miracle worker. You know: walks on water, changes water into wine, raises the dead. Between you and me, sister, your Rabbi needs to work on that end of the business."

Rachel buried her face in her robe. "You don't understand. The miracle wasn't in the resurrection. It was in *His* coming."

"Appears to me he came a little too late," Esther snorted.

"It's not *His* fault. It's mine. I lacked faith."

A gurgling noise came from a darkened space on the other side of the tent. Rachel looked at the unmoving lump on a mat. "Because of my lack of faith, this old woman and her son must suffer."

"You have nothing to reproach yourself for," Cassandra said. "It is because of you that this old woman saw the face of her son again. It is because of you that he walks among the living."

Esther coughed to conceal her laughter. "Princess, if you weren't blind you'd understand the horrible truth of your words."

Rachel crawled over to Sarah's pallet. "It is my doing that he is condemned to curse the daylight. If I had loved *Him* more —"

"You loved him enough to pray that he return from the grave," Cassandra interrupted.

A puzzled expression momentarily clouded Rachel's face. "No, not Lazarus, *Him*, my teacher. If I had loved Jeshua more and placed my total trust in Him then perhaps things would be different."

"If your Messiah is like my gods, then you bear no blame. My city was destroyed because of a wager between the gods. I was given the gift of prophecy from them, but at the same time the gods played the cruellest trick imaginable. Though I was permitted to foresee and relate the devastation of my nation, the gods ensured no one would believe me."

"Noah!" Esther exclaimed. "Sounds like your gods have the same sense of humour that Hashem does. Old Noah was commanded to build a big boat and tell the people that if they didn't repent of their wicked ways then a flood was coming that would wipe out the world. Noah did as he was told and Hashem saw to it that the people ignored him."

Rachel covered her ears. "I won't listen to you. My Saviour is kind. He does not play tricks on his followers. All He asks is love. And in return, Jeshua gives light to those who sit in darkness."

"We need to find this Messiah of yours." Cassandra stretched her arms in front of her and brought them back to her body, gathering up Rachel's dreams. "If he can truly make the lame to walk, the blind to see, then perhaps he can drive out the devils plaguing you. It's a journey worth taking. There is something to be gained from it for all of us."

"Is this an example of your sixth sense?" Esther asked.

"No, my common sense," Cassandra replied. "There is nothing holding us here."

A ghastly rattle escaped Sarah's throat. Her body arched into a bridge and flattened against the mat. Esther pushed Rachel away, lifted Sarah's arm by the wrist. When she released it, the skeletal limb dropped without a moan of protest from the old woman. "She's right. There's nothing keeping us here."

The camp slept while Lazarus listened to the mournful sound of the wind struggling to escape the canyon. Morning arrived accompanied by the angry shouts and curses of Barabbas and his men. Lazarus dashed into the camp without his robe. His appearance was marked by gales of laughter by the women tending the morning fires. Barabbas and a small gathering of men had congregated in front of Esther's tent.

Barabbas snatched a blanket from the hands of a woman exiting the tent. "For god sakes get decent," he said, tossing the blanket to Lazarus.

"What's going on?" Lazarus demanded.

"Gone, Cassandra, my sister, your wife, all gone. Your crazy woman convinced them to join her search for that Messiah of hers."

"You're a liar."

"That's true enough, but they are gone."

An old woman stirring the fire coals cackled, "They came near to waking the whole camp. Left chanting some nonsense about a man who calms the waters, causes the blind to see, and the lame to walk."

Lazarus stomped past the bandit and ripped down the flap of Esther's tent. Inside, Sarah's lifeless body was wrapped in a sheet of white cloth.

"Have a fig." Barabbas held out a shrivelled fruit. "For what it's worth, she passed on peacefully." The bandit draped his arm over

Lazarus. "There's nothing you can do but say a prayer and give her over to the worms."

Lazarus locked his arm around Barabbas' neck and flung him into a smouldering cooking fire. Barabbas rolled to his feet. He waved off his men from rushing to his aid. "She died without pain. That's something we all should be so lucky to do."

"God, how I envy her," Lazarus said.

"You're a bloody fool. You've been given a second chance to do whatever you didn't do in your first life."

"You forget. I've seen what exists on the other side."

"Describe it to me. Tell me what it looks like, smells like, sounds like. If it was so great, why was it so easy to bring you back from it?"

"You don't understand."

"You're damn right I don't understand. All I know is that together we could do big things, make a name for ourselves."

"I would rather not exist." Lazarus went back inside the tent. He came out carrying Sarah's limp body and fended off the efforts of Barabbas' men to take his mother from him. The men kept well behind him as he walked toward the end of the canyon. He placed Sarah on the ground, readjusting the sheet to cover her face.

With his bare hands, pulling away first fistfuls, then armloads of stone and earth, Lazarus tore at the wall of the canyon. By midday he had clawed out a hole large enough to hold two bodies. Clasping Sarah next to his chest, he crawled into the burrow.

Lazarus inhaled the gaseous emissions of decay while watching Sarah's corpse bloat under the winding sheet. He placed his ear next to her lips. He heard nothing. He ran his hands down her body in a futile attempt to feel her soul release itself from its mortal shell. He felt nothing. He knew it would take generations before she returned to dust. Yet he stood vigil for some would-be Messiah bent on resurrection.

The next morning Barabbas put a plate of food outside the cave. It remained untouched throughout the day. For six days the bandit repeated the ritual. Soon the stench of the decomposing body filled the camp. On the evening of the seventh day Lazarus emerged from the tomb. Barabbas held out a goatskin of wine. Lazarus drained the flask. He extended his hands to Barabbas and said, "Give me your sword."

The bandit withdrew his weapon from its scabbard, passing it to Lazarus blade first. Lazarus wrapped his fingers tightly around the sword. Its honed edge cut into his palm. Blood trickled down his wrist.

"I have to find Jeshua."

"First we have to find the women."

"They'll be with him."

"And then what?"

"There are three things I want from Jeshua." Lazarus slipped the sword between the folds of his robe and showed his palms. "Restore Rachel to her rightful mind. Make me whole again." The skin regenerated itself, closing around his wound. "And stop me from bringing grief and death to those around me."

Lazarus gazed at the crescent moon as it came even with the descending sun. Darkness enveloped the camp.

"Do you think Jeshua you will give you peace?"

He whirled around on hearing Cassandra's voice, but no one was there.

Rachel's laughter mocked him. "Why ask him? He's just an ignorant stonecutter."

Lazarus pressed the heels of his palms against his temples to drive out the voices of his tormentors. "Leave me alone."

He threw himself over Sarah's grave. "Mother!" He rested his head against the earth and rocks sealing her tomb. His plea was answered by a crow's cawing.

# 14

The Zealots assembled at the entrance of the canyon at dawn. Barabbas, dressed for the role of leader, wore a cuirass of tin scales. He had scraped the ensign of a Roman officer from the breastplate of the armour. Etched in its place was a nine-armed Menorah in commemoration of the Maccabees' victory over the Syrians. The design was replicated on his shield and on the greaves strapped around his calves.

Barabbas handed Lazarus a leather helmet and barked out an order to his men, "Move it! Get the lead out of your asses!"

The rebels quick-marched out of the canyon in single file. Two men raced ahead to scout the terrain. Two other men lagged behind to cover the band's flank. Barabbas kept his eyes trained on the cliffs and the rocks surrounding them. At irregular intervals he would come to an abrupt halt, and send one of his men dashing into the hills or around a bend.

"You remind me of an old woman," Lazarus griped. "At this pace we'll never get out of these hills."

"I'm not going to stumble into a trap and get myself killed because of your impatience to have a one-on-one with Jeshua."

"What a joke — the terrible Barabbas, scourge of Judea, is afraid of his own shadow."

"Time was when no Roman patrol would have had the guts to trespass into these hills."

"I thought you owned these mountains."

"That was before Pilate sent mercenaries from Gaul to clean us out. Before they made peace with Caesar, they held off the Romans for sixty years."

"It's going to take us that long to get out of here."

"If I wanted a nag I would have married one."

On the morning of the third day the Zealots stopped to eat and sleep. Barabbas climbed a ridge and peered off into the desert. A cloud of dust rose from the land about a mile away.

"Romans?" Lazarus asked.

Barabbas smirked. "If you're going to survive in this game you have to learn to read the signs. That cloud of dust is too wide, too thick to be caused by a patrol of soldiers. It's my guess that it's a clan of Bedouin herders. They must be on their way to Beersheba."

"How can you be so sure?"

"Because only a Bedouin would dare cross that open wasteland. And besides," Barabbas turned toward the East, "the Romans are over there." The glint of the sun ricocheting off polished metal disclosed the presence of a column of soldiers several leagues away. "They're moving too slowly to be a fighting unit." Barabbas leaned his shield against a quartz-and-mica–flecked boulder and unstrapped his greaves as he settled down to rest. Lazarus started to voice his frustration, but his words were drowned out by Barabbas' snoring.

At midday the men formed a circle and broke out the meagre rations they had brought with them in small clay pots suspended from their belts. Barabbas ladled out a mixture of ripe goat's cheese and mashed beans over a piece of bread. He rolled the bread around the fillings and stuffed the end into his mouth, grunting an invitation for Lazarus to share in his repast. The noise of twenty famished men smacking their lips and belching was loud enough to be heard in the desert below. A yard of wine was passed around the circle. Barabbas gulped a mouthful to wash away the sour taste of a meal that was only hours away from sprouting legs and walking off on its own.

"Here, drink. It will bring some colour to your face." Barabbas pinched Lazarus' cheek and dropped the wine sack into his lap. "Damn it, liven up, man. My men are nervous enough without you sitting there like death's second cousin."

Lazarus passed the wine sack along without drinking. "I've been thinking."

"That's a bad habit."

"It's wrong of me to drag you and your men along with me."

"I really don't give a damn about your mission." The outlaw guzzled another throat of wine when the goatskin passed his way. He flipped his shield over and tightened its arm strap.

"Then why are you going?"

"I told you when we first met, I'm a patriot."

"You also told me you were a thief, a liar and a murderer."

"Men who believe in a cause are a little of all those things," Barabbas said as he refastened his greaves. "I want to see if the mystic stands with us or against us."

Lazarus descended the hill and surveyed the desert. The sand dunes, constantly shifting and of changing form and size, rolled toward him like huge breakers on an ocean which knew no boundaries.

A black figure mounted on a grey horse appeared on the horizon. The rider's cape billowed in the wind like the wings of a great bat. The horseman did not use his bridle to control the galloping horse. He pressed his thighs into the animal's body to guide it toward its destination. When the rider was within fifty yards of Lazarus he dismounted in one motion. The rider ran toward Lazarus with his arms open to embrace him. Lazarus felt for the handle of his sword, withdrawing its blade a foot from its scabbard. Before the horseman reached Lazarus, Barabbas' men charged out of the hills and tackled him.

A huge bearded face hovered over the man. "And what do we have here?" Barabbas asked.

The man got up, placed his hand over his heart and bowed his head. "Salaam, peace be with you and your children. Peace always be with you."

"If it is the will of Allah." Barabbas made a half-hearted effort of returning the gesture. "And I'm not so sure that it is."

There was something familiar about the Bedouin's voice. Lazarus jerked off the scarf concealing the man's identity. "Hajid!"

"I see you are keeping more esteemed company these days, old friend."

"Don't call me friend."

"After what we have been through together, what else can I call you but friend?"

Barabbas jabbed Hajid with the butt end of his knife. "You know this Bedouin?"

"I know him."

Hajid slipped around Barabbas to hug Lazarus. "It is good to see you. You are looking well, as well as one can expect you to look."

Lazarus lashed out at the Bedouin, "Where is Kalil?"

"He is no longer with me."

"I suppose you dissolved your partnership."

"Kalil is my brother."

"Get on your horse and ride back to wherever you came from."

"My business is not with you." Hajid turned his back on Lazarus. "It is with the great and terrible Barabbas."

Barabbas strutted back and forth. "I like this man."

"Greatness is in your blood." Hajid's hands flew into the air, touching the ground as he bowed from the waist. "One day men will write songs about how you saw the opportunity to reach your goal and seized it."

Lazarus inserted himself between Hajid and Barabbas. "I don't trust him."

Barabbas frowned. "Go think about what you'll do when you meet the carpenter. This man and I have business to discuss."

Hajid placed his scimitar on the ground. Barabbas put his own weapon next to Hajid's sword, but left his dagger tucked into the belt of his robe. The two brigands lowered themselves onto the sand, watching each other warily.

Barabbas spoke first. "You know our language very well."

"I speak many languages."

Lazarus stood behind Hajid. "Don't listen to him. The bastard speaks every language but the truth."

The Bedouin spread out his robe like a great pair of wings. He reached inside it and removed a small cloth bag. He turned the bag over, spilling out a handful of gold coins. "A gift for you. A token of the bond we hope to form with your people."

Barabbas picked up one coin and bent it between his fingers. "We speak the same language."

"We are both children of Abraham."

"But different mothers," Barabbas replied.

"What has passed is past." Hajid looked up as a flash of light bouncing off metal crossed the sky. "Our mutual enemy is out there. We are slaves of a foreign power."

"Why should a petty column of Roman soldiers concern me?"

"Because they have something we both want."

"Get to the point."

"Four days ago a press-gang of Roman slavers captured some of my people who had gone ahead of us to search for better grazing land."

"What has this got to do with us?" Lazarus asked.

"Kalil was among those captured."

"That's your problem."

Barabbas threw a furious look at Lazarus. "He's our guest." He stressed the last word and turned to address Hajid. "But your problem, as tragic as it is, is your problem."

"We want you to help us free our people."

"I have to admit, you have nerve."

Hajid walked to his horse. "It was not by accident that we sought you out." He untied a carpet secured to his saddle and unrolled it in front of Barabbas. Inside the carpet was a crudely fashioned crutch and a brooch.

Barabbas picked up the crutch and thrust the forked end into the Bedouin's throat, pinning him to the ground. "What have you done to them?"

Hajid rasped, "They are safe. We found them wandering across the desert half dead from exhaustion and thirst."

Barabbas flung the crutch away and helped the Bedouin to his feet. "Forgive me for my lack of hospitality."

"Of course I do not expect you to help us without some form of compensation." Hajid rubbed his throat. "Where there are slavers, there is gold."

Barabbas shrugged. "We can take the gold without you."

"You could, but at what price?"

Lazarus kept his silence. His mind was fixed on the image of Rachel and Cassandra held against their will in Hajid's camp.

"Come with me and speak with my Sheik."

Barabbas picked up the purse of gold coins, juggling its weight in his hand. "Take your sword. We'll follow you."

# 15

The tents of Hajid's people came into view as the Zealots descended one last sand dune. The Bedouin camp was laid out next to a dead river bed. Beyond the main body of shelters was a large tent. A red pennant flew from the support pole protruding through its roof. Women went in and out of the tent carrying baskets of rags on top of their heads.

Barabbas said, "I didn't know you kept your women segregated from the men."

"Our laws are the same as yours." Hajid was annoyed. "Women who have started their cycle of life must remain apart from their husbands until they are considered clean."

Immense clay water jugs stood in the centre of the encampment. The jugs were guarded by two men who crouched over a polished wooden board. Seven small depressions were scooped out on each side of the board. At either end were large pockets. The water wardens took turns tossing a single die. They picked up the number of stones indicated by the throw of the die and moved them around the board, dropping a stone in each hole.

"Melchior!" Hajid called out as he kicked off his sandals and approached a white tent that formed the nucleus of the camp.

Two bodyguards bearing staffs topped with crescent moons escorted an ancient man out of the tent. His delicate fingers trickled down the gold chains dangling around his neck until they touched a disk in the shape of the sun. He lifted the medallion. Hajid kissed it.

Melchior's waist-length platinum beard stood in blinding contrast to his saffron-coloured robe. "It is good to see you've returned safely and have brought friends with you." Despite the decrepit frame, the voice of the chieftain was powerful. He crooked his finger at Lazarus.

"Magi, this is the man I have told you about."

"And the other?"

Barabbas moved forward. The bodyguards closed ranks, formed a barrier, blocking him off from Melchior.

"He and his men will help us to get our people back."

The old man adjusted a tall mitre, emblazoned with silver chimaeras, gryphons and other mythical beasts, which kept slipping over his shrunken head. "I suppose it was necessary to ask him to join us. Even Lord Zurvan had to make a pact with demons once to save the world from darkness." His gaze fell on Lazarus. "Was your journey difficult?"

"Hajid knew the way."

"Not that journey. The great one. The one all must take, but from which few return."

"The Lord is our light and salvation," Rachel's crystal voice sang out from Melchior's tent.

Lazarus tried to break past Melchior but his path was obstructed by the bodyguards. The old man's fingers closed around Lazarus' wrist as Rachel led Cassandra out of the tent. They were dressed in kaftans the same colour as Melchior's robe. Rachel smiled at Lazarus. He felt a profound sense of loneliness. Esther wobbled behind them on a newly carved ivory leg.

"I read your tale in the stars." Melchior released Lazarus. "You are the dead one who walks among the living."

"You can see that I am alive."

"Appearances can be deceiving."

Again Lazarus tried to get around Melchior but stopped when the old man placed his hands on his shoulders and said, "They are indeed beautiful." Cassandra and Rachel went back into the tent. One of the bodyguards led a splendid black stallion over to Melchior.

"I love beautiful things." Melchior tenderly ran his hand over the neck of the animal. "Horses, gold..." He lifted the medallion from around his neck and let it fall against his hollow chest. "And especially women."

"I can appreciate that," Barabbas joined in.

Melchior took the reins of the stallion from the guard and held them out to Lazarus. "What price do you want for your women?"

"They're not mine to sell. They are free."

"There is no such thing as a free man, much less a free woman. We all belong to someone or something."

"I told you they're not for sale."

"Then perhaps I will take them."

"Perhaps you'll try."

"This is ridiculous." Barabbas' hand slipped into the band of his girdle and clutched the pommel of his dagger. He circled behind Hajid.

"You find this situation amusing?" Melchior asked.

"Of course it's funny. You're ready to sacrifice a good horse and a faithful soldier for a blind whore and a madwoman." Barabbas gasped when Hajid rammed his hip into the outlaw's pelvis and flipped him over his shoulder.

Melchior sighed. "If he can fight no better than that, we are indeed in trouble."

"Whoa, he caught me off guard," Barabbas protested. The bodyguards stood over the bandit with their scimitars poised above his head.

"Enough of this stupidity. Let him up," Melchior said. "Our battle is not with you, it is with the Romans who have conquered your people and enslaved my friends."

Barabbas slapped the dust off himself. "Since when does a sheik refer to his followers as his friends?"

"If it were not for their kindness to a stranger lost in this inhospitable wilderness, I would not be here today," Melchior replied as he walked to his tent flanked by his bodyguards. "You and your companions must be tired. Rest and we will talk over dinner."

The water wardens had continued playing stones during the confrontation between Hajid and Barabbas. After Melchior disappeared into his tent, Hajid thumped them on their heads. "Mehmed, Buttra, stop your stupid game and pour a bath for our guests." Grumbling, they uncoiled themselves. They grabbed a handle on each side of a water jug and lugged it across the camp, placing it behind a carpet strung out between two posts.

"I thought you Bedouin treasure water above gold," Lazarus remarked.

"We do," Hajid answered. "But Melchior is not a Bedouin."

"His followers are."

"When Kalil and I stumbled into this camp after fleeing Revivim, I believed I was a Bedouin. After spending time with Melchior, I am no longer certain who I was or what I have become."

"Bathing is a waste of water, but if that's what it takes to get a meal around here..." Barabbas muttered as he plodded toward the curtain.

"I thought you were sitting pretty in Revivim," Lazarus told Hajid while waiting his turn to bathe.

"Najar found out that the Romans were offering a reward for information leading to the arrest of the men who killed their soldiers."

"She turned you in?"

"In fairness to her, she sent her slave ahead of the patrol to warn me they were coming. That's my story."

"What about Melchior? What brought him here?"

"That's his story. You'll have to ask him."

Barabbas strolled past Lazarus. "Not to worry, there's plenty of water left for you. I only used a handful."

Barabbas' men remained on the edge of the camp. They watched the Bedouin warriors practice leaping on their horses and charging across the dried river bed, pointing barbed lances in front of them. In unison the Bedouin pulled on the reins of their mounts and came to a halt a few meters away from Barabbas' men.

Weary of the Bedouin's game of intimidation, the Zealots demonstrated their own martial skills to these bastard children of

Abraham. They dashed between the line of horses, swinging their swords, pounding on their shields as they whooped, "Hear, oh Israel. God is One."

The guardians of the water grinned. It was evident that the motley band of Jews were no match for their warriors. But what they were unaware of was that the Zealots, like the Maccabees before them, were masters of stealth. They appeared out of nowhere and vanished after launching swift attacks calculated to send fear and confusion through their foes' ranks.

At nightfall Lazarus and Barabbas were summoned to Melchior. He did not greet them when they entered his dwelling. He sat with his legs crossed, his feet folded under him.

"Ohm." A hollow sound born in Melchior's belly drifted toward them. His eyes were closed. He held his arms above his head. The pads of his forefingers and thumbs touched. His body was naked save for a dhoti, a white piece of cloth worn like a diaper covering his lower body. Gradually he opened his eyes and stared into space, apparently unaware of their presence. He exhaled. "Welcome." His eyes came into focus. Melchior spread his arms out. The bodyguards held his saffron robe between them and helped him on with it.

"What was that noise you were making when we came in?" Lazarus asked.

"Noise? Oh yes, 'Ohm.' It's nothing. Years ago I accompanied my people in their conquest of a land beyond the Indus River. Despite the fact that the country was thoroughly defeated, its holy men maintained a kind of serene dignity, a noble acceptance of their lot. From them I learned to meditate. Ohm was their key to opening the portal of inner peace and locking the door of trivial earthly concerns."

"Never heard of this Indus." Barabbas glanced around the stark interior of the tent. It was bare except for a rug that covered its floor and a few pillows. In one corner an open chest overflowed with sheepskin scrolls turning brown with age.

"I doubt if they have ever heard of this scrap of wasteland either," Melchior retorted. "I tried to learn about their culture and religion. It was far too complicated. Too many gods, too many nuances for me to understand."

"Some people I know would say that the hand of our Lord played a role in their downfall. Adonai has a habit of punishing those who worship false gods." Barabbas quoted from memory, "For our God is a jealous God. All nations must bend their knees before Him."

"If this is true, where is your empire?"

"How should I know?"

"You shouldn't."

The women entered the tent bearing trays of food. They placed the trays on the rug and knelt. Barabbas, seeing the platters full of dried dates, millet paste, bread and meat, lunged for the victuals.

"Restrain yourself," Melchior said. "It is my custom to allow the women the honour of first tasting the food."

Barabbas frowned when he caught sight of his sister smirking. "Then eat, damn it."

The guards handed Melchior a platter. "It is not the eating that is important. It is the offering which is significant."

"Start offering. I haven't eaten anything since yesterday," Barabbas complained.

"If you shut up, maybe we can get through this tonight," Lazarus snapped at the bandit.

"Generally, this offering is done with a spirit of generosity and compassion," Melchior groaned. "But, seeing as you are sorely deficient in those areas, I will expedite matters for you."

"Yeah, generosity, compassion," Barabbas said. "Just get on with it. Okay?"

"Ahura Mazda, upon creating the universe, graced it with the presence of Mithra, the first woman, who gave birth to the earth." Melchior held out a tray to Rachel. He waited for her to take a date before moving on to Cassandra and Esther. "Man, Ahura Mazda's other creation, though powerful and innovative, was greedy. He did not care what pain he inflicted upon the living body of this planet. It was in woman that Ahura Mazda placed the heart of the world. For the creator knew that protected within woman's bosom his creation would thrive and flourish."

Barabbas tried to sneak a fruit off the tray as it passed by him but had his hand slapped for his trouble.

Esther stuffed a date in her mouth. She showed it to Barabbas while chewing. "I'm getting used to this," she taunted him.

Melchior took a tray from one of his bodyguards. He chanted as he moved back and forth between the three women. "From the womb of Mithra sprang the Amesha Spentas, seven daughters, to help her tend and nurse this new world." They used their fingers to scoop out millet paste from the bowl he offered them.

"What are you seeking, my son?" Melchior asked as he turned to Lazarus.

Lazarus thrust his disfigured face inches from the old man's nose. "Don't call me your son."

"You are my son. Just as I am your son. Just as man is the son of God and God the son of man. It is my belief that our existence is the product of our ability to create not only ourselves but everything around us, including the universe and the creator we have dreamed and who has dreamed us."

"If I am the product of your dreams then your existence must be a nightmare."

Barabbas could stomach the philosophising no longer and belched. "You got any wine?" A guard tossed a goatskin into his lap.

"If you ask me, you got side-tracked from your quest," Barabbas said, gulping the wine and waving his arm above his head. "Doesn't seem like you can do a lot of soul-searching while leading this bunch and living in a tent."

"It is the detour in one's life that brings one closer to why he embarked on the journey in the first place." Melchior closed his eyes as he recalled his past. "Thirty-three years ago, I entered this land with two of my fellow scholars in search of the meaning of a magnificent celestial phenomenon. One night a brilliant object appeared in the heavens which moved in an arch across the western sky. We predicted

119

that if we followed the path of the star we would find the centre of our dreams. Once locating the master dream we could make it dream of a universe free of evil.

"Our search was fruitless." Melchior sighed deeply. "We followed the progression of the star to your land. My nation was at war with Rome at the time, so we masqueraded as traders to avoid being captured as spies. We brought along a few bolts of cloth with gold coins sewn into the fabric, and frankincense and myrrh. For five months we travelled through this desolate country, stopping in every village along the way to recast our celestial charts. One night we entered Bayt Lahm. We thought it was just another one of the destitute collections of houses that are scattered through Judea like bird droppings. We were wrong. The town was teeming with people who had come to be counted in the Roman census.

"Soldiers patrolled the village. We knew if we were stopped and searched the Romans would wonder why three traders who spoke the local language so poorly would be carrying zodiac charts and maps with them. We tried to find somewhere to hide. Finally we located a cave that was used as a stable behind an inn. Unfortunately, there was already someone in it, a woman and man. The woman had just given birth to a boy child. She badgered her husband to throw us out. I protested that there was no place else to go. She insisted the cave wasn't big enough for the animals and us. Finally, Balthazar went to our camels. He returned with some of the goods we had brought along. After a bit of haggling the woman and her husband agreed to let us stay. What we did not foresee was that in the morning they would leave before us and advise the owner of the stable of our presence."

Melchior's chest heaved as he recounted the end of his story. "When Balthazar and Gaspar went outside to tend to our animals they saw six Roman centurions marching toward them. They screamed my name. Perhaps it was a plea for me to come to their aid or a warning for me to flee. It was really not much of a contest, words against swords. I escaped by burrowing into a pile of dung.

"When it grew dark I fled Bayt Lahm. My cowardice clung to me worse than the stench of the dung heap. I resolved to die in the desert, but these Bedouin stumbled upon me and rescued me." Melchior clasped Lazarus' hand and pulled him closer. "Ahura Mazda saved me just as he saved you for some purpose neither one of us understands. We both must discover how our chain of existence is linked to the great dream."

"The more I hear, the less sure I am that I want to join his men," Barabbas said. "I'm worried that when the time comes to fight, the only hint we'll have of where they have fled to is the smell of the farts they leave behind them."

Melchior spread millet paste on a wedge of flat bread, wrapped it around a charcoal-burned piece of goat meat and gave it to Barabbas. "Hajid and his horsemen would be very glad to challenge your proposition." The guards squeezed Barabbas between them and jostled the bandit to the door.

Melchior brushed his hand against Lazarus' cheek. "My days of dreaming are nearly over. Yours are just beginning."

Melchior walked to the front of the tent. He slipped his arm through Barabbas' arm. "Your friend and I will meet with Hajid to plan our strategy against the Romans."

Esther got up to follow her brother. "I guess it's as good a time as any to tell him," she mumbled. She had decided to remain with the Bedouin. Barabbas could go back to sleeping with dogs and eating rotten meat. She had found her Promised Land.

Lazarus tore off a piece of bread with his teeth. He chewed without tasting his food, glaring at Rachel and Cassandra. He tossed the half-eaten bread onto the platter and pushed himself off the rug. "I'll sleep outside."

Rachel clung to his robe. "Don't go, we have to talk."

"If it's another one of your rants about the carpenter, keep it to yourself."

Though the blood raced to her cheeks, Rachel maintained her calm. "Not about the Saviour, it's you who I have to talk about."

"That subject doesn't interest me either."

"Listen to her," Cassandra said.

"Listen to what, more demented professions of faith?"

Lazarus kissed Rachel's cheek. "So much for her undying affection," he said as she turned her face away from him.

"Tomorrow morning I'm leaving." Lazarus threw open the tent flap. "You and this blind oracle can do what you want."

"I am staying with Melchior. He believes in my vision," Cassandra responded.

Rachel ran out of the tent ahead of Lazarus and stood in his path. "I'm going with you."

Lazarus' voice turned as sharp and cold as splintered glass. "I'll find your Messiah and make him right the misery his miracle has caused."

"No, we'll find Him together."

"That's your choice," Lazarus said.

# 16

The Roman slave caravan slogged laboriously across the desert, its progress impeded by the lumbering line of prisoners chained together by their feet. At the head of the slave train, an officer rode a dappled gelding. He looked behind him at the foot soldiers prodding the slaves along with spears.

The monotony of the routine was broken when a slave stumbled, dragging the men in front and in back of him to the ground. A soldier uncoiled his cat-o'-nine-tails and flogged the prisoner until he struggled to his feet, his back torn by the metal barbs at the end of the leather thongs.

"Marcus, enough!"

"Have you seen what's in store for this poor bastard in the copper mines, Flavius? If I were to kill him now he would bless me."

"Our job is to get them there alive."

"I hate this." Marcus slapped the handle of his whip against his thigh. "I am a soldier, not a slaver." He flung the whip into the desert.

The officer jerked the reins of his horse and rode over to Marcus. "Sandstorm?" he asked, pointing at a curtain of dust moving their way.

Marcus unsheathed his sword. "I don't think so, it's moving too fast. Doesn't cover enough space to be a storm."

"What then?" The officer's question was answered before he could return to the head of the caravan. Out of the cloud galloped fifty black-robed horsemen, shattering the stillness of the desert with their war cries.

"Stand your ground, men!" The officer dug his heels into the side of his mount and charged the warriors riding down on them. He passed beween two Bedouin whirling their swords over their heads. His horse pulled up, reversed its direction and trotted back to the caravan with the decapitated body of its master.

Marcus grabbed hold of the bridle. He shoved the headless body out of the saddle and mounted the horse. "Leave the prisoners!"

"The captain said to stand our ground," Flavius objected.

"Don't be a fool!" Marcus bellowed. "We have to get out of the open. Make for the hills."

The soldiers abandoned the slaves and raced after Marcus. Flavius glanced over his shoulder. The Bedouin had ceased their assault to free their brethren.

"Get into the rocks before they regroup," Marcus ordered. "They can't follow us in on their horses." The soldiers scrambled up the hill, seeking cover behind the large boulders on the lower slope.

Several minutes passed before the Bedouin remounted. Forming a perfect line, they cantered toward the Romans. When they were within a hundred yards of the soldiers they stopped. Hajid swung his legs over the side of his horse and sat sidesaddle. "Throw down your weapons and come down; no harm will come to you." An arrow flew past his head. "Have it your way." The Bedouin horses retreated out of the archers' range.

"They think they can wait us out," Marcus told Flavius. "When it gets dark we'll make our way up these hills and escape on the other side. In the meanwhile I'll tell the bowmen to make sure they keep their distance."

"You love this, don't you?" Flavius asked.

Marcus' reply remained trapped in his throat. A stone whizzed through the air, embedding itself between his eyes. He toppled backwards. The chant of "God is One!" erupted from the boulders above him as his body rolled to the bottom of the hill.

Flavius looked at the terrain surrounding him. He watched helplessly as Barabbas' men appeared from behind the rocks. The archers twisted around to take aim but it was too late. They were bombarded with a rain of stone missiles. The Romans, refusing to submit to humiliation at the hands of these barbarians, rose to their feet. Some of them dashed up the hill to confront the Zealots, while others raced down to engage the Bedouin horsemen in battle. The outcome was pre-ordained.

Flavius trudged dumbly up the hill past the fallen bodies of his comrades. As he lifted his sword, he was felled by a hard blow to the back of his head.

"Stay put, don't move." Lazarus towered over Flavius and rolled him onto his belly.

Though he could not see what was going on around him, Flavius heard screams of anguish. Wounded soldiers, not fortunate enough to be killed in the initial attack, were disembowelled and left writhing in their own excrement and viscera. Lazarus remained standing above Flavius, a guardian angel in the guise of a demon.

Barabbas came over to Lazarus. In his hands he held the bloody testicles of a Roman soldier. The bandit booted Flavius in his ribs. Flavius stifled a cry of pain.

"Roll this one over. Let's see what kind of balls he has on him."

Hajid called out from the plain below, "This is what you came for." He held up a saddlebag taken from the Roman officer's horse. He turned it upside down, pouring out its contents of gold and silver. Barabbas ran down the hill to retrieve the coins before they were lost in the sand.

Crouching next to Flavius, Lazarus whispered, "Wait until dark, then leave."

The young soldier lifted his head and saw Rachel standing at the crown of the hill, from which point she had watched the carnage take place.

"Don't blame God for the work of men," she wept.

Night came. The solemn chant of the Zealots burying their dead tortured Flavius as he slithered on his stomach through the mutilated corpses of his fellow soldiers.

Hidden behind some boulders, Lazarus watched over the soldier. He stepped from his cover when he was certain Flavius had made good his escape.

Rachel called after Lazarus, "Come, sleep. We leave for Nazareth in the morning."

Lazarus stood at the top of the hill, his silhouette pasted against the moon. "It means nothing to me." He surveyed the ground below him. The Zealot's campfire had burned down to a red glow.

Rachel's voice vibrated with excitement. "It is the home of Jeshua."

Lazarus vanished over the ridge. He wandered through the rocky terrain. Finally hc found himself in a barren clearing on a hilltop as flat as a table. Thirteen stone monoliths worn smooth by the elements were arranged in a circle. Barely visible on their polished surfaces were ancient prayers dedicated by the original Canaanite inhabitants of Israel to their pantheon of nature gods. These gods came before Abraham's jealous deity urging Joshua to slay to the last child the race of the idolaters.

Lazarus slumped to his knees in front of the largest monolith. He threw back his head and howled, reached out to claw the face of the moon. "Just who is this Jeshua? In whose name does he claim the power?"

"Whatever power he has is not of his making," a voice rose from behind the stone column. Lazarus drew his dagger as he rolled out of the shadow that fell across him.

"Put that away," a hunch-backed little man swinging his arms like a monkey ordered.

"Hungry?" The man held out two closed fists. "Go on, guess." A rough strip of camel hide still bearing its fur was tied around his waist. "Choose." He shook his fists impatiently. Lazarus tapped his right hand. The man hopped around, singing, "You're wrong, you're wrong." He uncurled his fingers, revealing a dirty but empty palm. "It's in this one," he chortled, as he slowly opened his other fist, plucked out a locust by its wings and dropped it into his mouth. "Can't talk now. I'm eating."

The man's body was coated with filth and pitted with festering ulcers. His stench was worse than the smell of the grave. His hair had grown so long that it was interwoven with his knee-length beard. Only the green eyes retained a spark of humanity. They shone through his tangled mass of hair like two candles illuminating a dark room. The man picked a fly, feeding on his open sores, from his chest. He popped the insect into his mouth.

"John, my name's John. Though most people call me the Baptist, if they speak of me at all." He wiped his palm on his camel skin apron and reached out to shake Lazarus' hand. "Reckon you're looking for my cousin."

"Cousin?"

"Second cousin actually, on my mother's side."

The Baptist spat, working it into the earth with his bare foot. "I haven't seen Jeshua since I baptised him at the River Jordan. It is better that I never see his blasphemous face again. Then he knew God. Now he thinks he is God."

John dropped to his haunches and lunged for a cricket. "I haven't eaten for days," he excused himself, stuffing the insect into his mouth. He chewed slowly and swallowed before mimicking Lazarus. "In whose name does he claim the power? I like it. It has a righteous sound to it. Perhaps I'll use it when or if I go back to the cities to preach." John the Baptist reclined on the earth, crossing his arms behind his head. "Didn't mean to, but I couldn't help overhearing you. I saw you coming and hid behind one of these heathen stones. I thought you might be one of Herod's men."

"Well, do you have an answer?" Lazarus' hand darted out and snatched a bug flying past. He gave it to the Baptist.

John crushed the insect under his molars. "Is it important?"

"For me it is."

"His power is power. It feeds off the faith of those who believe in him just as fire feeds off wood. I confess that I played no small part in adding fuel to the flames at the River Jordan. It was one of my best sermons, a miracle of sorts."

"What kind of answer did I expect from a bug eater?" Lazarus muttered as he walked away.

"Don't go." Like one of the small lizards scampering around the monoliths, John covered the distance between Lazarus and himself on his hands and knees. "It's been months since I've spoken with another human being." He wrapped his arms around Lazarus' legs. "I'll answer your question directly. He gets his power from me."

Lazarus tried to shake off the lunatic but stopped when John said, "And from you, from his disciples, from the masses who gather to hear him speak, from everyone in the world who craves a miracle to affirm the existence of something greater than themselves. You see, individually we are too weak to make even a small miracle. But when we channel our energy collectively, direct it through a person who craves the power, we can work any miracle."

"Even the raising of the dead?"

"Positively, if for no other reason than to prove death is not final."

Lazarus helped the Baptist to his feet. "It's too cold for you up here. Come with me to my camp and I'll get you some real food."

"I thought it would be obvious to you. I'm hiding. I got a trifle over-enthusiastic during one of my sermons. I began by attacking Herod's association with the Romans and before I could stop myself I indicted him of incest. I guess if I had stopped there things might have cooled down. But I was on a roll." The Baptist began unknotting his beard. "Before I realised it, I charged Herod and his bitch with every indecency short of cracking their cheeks and inviting Pontius Pilate to bugger them with the Torah." John shivered when a gust of wind blew over his body. "The word reached me that Herod was a bit miffed. I decided to hide up here until things calmed down." He sighed. "What can I do? Preaching is an addiction. Once the spirit takes over I can't stop."

Lazarus unfastened the leather doublet covering his robe. "You better put this on. It's not much but it may keep you a little warmer at night."

The hairy little man slipped his arms through the armour's holes. He caressed the hard leather. "Don't tell anyone you've seen me."

"Not even your cousin?"

"Cousin! He's worse than Herod. At least that apostate is conscious of his treachery. Jeshua thinks you can serve God while wearing the yoke of the infidels."

By the time Lazarus arrived back at camp, the sun had been up for two hours. Barabbas and his men had packed their gear and were getting ready to leave.

Lazarus took Rachel's pack from her. He reached inside and removed a round of bread and a pot of cheese.

"You had us worried," she said.

"I was in the hills thinking about how everything remotely linked to your Messiah leads to the grave."

"Barabbas says we have to make it to Nazareth before the Romans send out patrols to hunt for their missing men."

"Go join the others. I'll catch up with you later."

Lazarus nibbled at the pita as he watched the bandits and Rachel descend the hills and head north to Nazareth. He did not want them to witness his placing the bread and cheese on a rock. He glanced up at the crest of the hill and thought he saw the ape-like body of the Baptist scurrying among the boulders.

# 17

The Zealots left the crude trail they had been walking on for days and stepped onto a cobble road constructed by the Romans. Milestones indicated how far it was between the small military outposts spread out along the road and the central garrison in Jerusalem. The markers were destined to be defaced. The civilising influence of Rome, its notably superior system of roads, law, architecture and agriculture, was abhorrent to virtually every Jew, regardless of their political or religious stance. These contributions of Rome toward improving the lot of Judea's inhabitants cast doubt on the primacy of Israel's God.

Barabbas removed his backpack and sat on it. "Over that knoll is your Messiah's hometown."

"Let's get going then," Lazarus said and took Rachel's hand.

Barabbas pointed at the scarf around Lazarus' neck. "Keep your face covered. Anonymity is the key to survival." The bandit lay down, using the backpack as a pillow.

"Aren't you coming?"

"No, you go along on your own. I'll catch up with you later. I have some business to deal with first."

Rachel and Lazarus found their way to the centre of the village. Nazareth reeked of sour wine, bad meat, and vomit. Derelicts staggered in and out of the numerous taverns, the village's primary source of revenue. A kilometre away from Nazareth stood the only sign of opulence in the destitute environs, a three-storey, rose-coloured hostel.

Transparent mauve curtains breathed in and out as the wind blew through the building's unshuttered windows.

Rachel licked her lips when she saw a woman lowering a hollowed-out gourd into a well. "Please, could I have a drink of your water?"

The woman did not answer. She kept her back to Rachel.

"Just a sip would do." Rachel was again greeted with silence.

"She asked for water." Lazarus grabbed the gourd and handed it to Rachel.

"I don't share my water with harlots." The woman's milky eyes showed through the dark veil concealing her face.

Lazarus hooked his fingers under the top of his scarf and pulled it below his cadaverous smile. "A son of this village brought me back from the grave."

"The one who summoned you from Sheol also calls us to him." The woman gathered the bottom of her veil, rolling it slowly up to her forehead. The ulcerated pulp of her leprous face oozed yellow pus.

"Drink, dear, drink all you want," she cackled.

"If my Lord can eat with sinners, and dispense His grace to all, including lepers, then who am I to refuse the water which comes from His own well?" said Rachel.

Lazarus knocked the gourd out of Rachel's hands as she raised it to her lips. "Now I understand why everyone survives on wine around here."

Eleven lepers in different stages of the disease lumbered toward the well. One man, propelling his legless body with his stiff arms, held up the stubs of his hands. "Why are you here? Who are you looking for?"

They continued creeping toward Lazarus like half-formed crabs.

"I've come to find Jeshua."

"We're waiting for him, too." The leper scratched his nose with his stump. "He has to come home eventually. And when he does, we'll greet him with the loudest hallelujah he has ever heard."

The woman from the well joined in, "And when he does, he'll give us the cure and we'll be whole again."

"See, they believe in Him." Rachel ran to embrace the woman. "He is the one whose coming was foretold."

"Get off me!" the woman shrieked.

"Yetta doesn't like to be touched. She's worried something might fall off," the legless man said.

Lazarus encircled Rachel's waist and pulled her from Yetta. "If I wanted to find out about Jeshua where should I go?"

The leper lifted his stub and wagged it at a windowless hovel.

Lazarus steered Rachel toward the wretched dwelling.

"Shush." Rachel cocked her head. "Something's missing."

"What?"

"Can't you hear it?"

"Hear what?" Lazarus pushed the door of the hovel open.

"The silence." Rachel looked at the sky, then up and down the empty street. "Not a sound, not so much as the buzzing of flies."

Cat-like green eyes absorbed the light flooding the rancid smelling house. "Who needs flies when you have swarms of lepers?" There was something vaguely familiar about the voice.

"Find a chair and make yourselves comfortable." Their host's thick red hair protruded like straw from under an Egyptian charioteer's helmet.

"What kept you? We never thought you'd get here." Barabbas pulled his robe together as he walked through a curtain at the rear of the room.

"I hear you're looking for my brother." The red-haired man sat at a table littered with empty wine jugs and crusts of bread. "Nidavah, get in here and clean up this mess!"

A woman with a thin blanket wrapped around her naked body pushed aside the curtain Barabbas had passed through. "I'm your whore, not your maid." She crossed the room and picked up a half-full wine goblet and returned to her sleeping chamber, pulling the curtain closed behind her.

Lazarus glared at Barabbas. "What kind of joke is this?"

"James is one of us, a Zealot," Barabbas said. "We served together for awhile under the Bar Kochba."

"You've known Jeshua's brother all the time and never bothered to tell me?"

"It slipped my mind. I'm not in the habit of talking about members of our underground."

James strode up to Lazarus and said, "I lost touch with my brother a long time ago."

Rachel crawled in front of Lazarus and clutched the hem of James' robe. "Those who have witnessed the calling of our Saviour to His mission are truly blessed in the sight of God."

"Get up." James rolled his eyes. "Most of the villagers here despise Jeshua more than Herod and his Roman masters."

Rachel released James' garment. "There is no way you could have sprung from the same womb as He who has brought the gift of light to the world."

"You should have sold your crazy wife when you had a chance," Barabbas muttered under his breath.

James pulled down the cloth covering Lazarus' face. "Some miracle."

Barabbas draped his arms over both their necks. "You two should really get to know each other, open up, introduce your families to one another."

Lazarus slipped out from under Barabbas' arm. "My family is dead."

"Oops, that's right." The bandit, pressing his palms together, faced James. "Both your parents are alive, aren't they?"

"Quit asking questions you already know the answer to," James said.

"Go on, introduce them to Mary and Joseph so they can see what noble lineage your brother springs from."

Lazarus nudged Barabbas out of the way. "I need to find Jeshua."

"Even if he were here, I doubt if he could help you." James surveyed Lazarus' face, studying every detail, from the stone eye to the colourless smile drawn back across the teeth in a death's-head grin.

Rachel burst out in song. "Hail Mary, mother of our Saviour. Blessed be she among all women."

"So she wants to meet Jeshua's saintly mother, does she?" James sneered, squinting into the harsh sunlight pouring through the open door. "Then, damn it, follow me."

"Go on," Barabbas cajoled. "He's taking you to the source of the legend."

Lazarus helped Rachel to her feet. "Are you coming?" he asked Barabbas.

"No, I'm staying here." Barabbas nodded at the curtain. "Nidavah and I have some unfinished business."

"Hail Mary, mother of Jeshua. Blessed be her among all women." Rachel whirled across the room and out into the street.

When they reached the gates of the city, James cut across the countryside and hiked toward the rose-coloured building.

"Ever since the hordes of lepers, cripples and women of all types, from the virtuous to the wanton, have swarmed here to await the appearance of their Master, the villagers have refused to acknowledge my mother's establishment as part of Nazareth."

"That's wise," Rachel whispered. "Our Lord has many enemies."

When they arrived at the house, James picked up a mallet and struck a brass gong hanging on a post. An intricate depiction of King David dancing before the ark of the covenant was carved on the massive double doors of the building. James beat the gong again.

Rachel slid her feet out of her sandals. She jabbed her finger in Lazarus' ribs. "This is holy ground; take off your shoes."

"Keep your sandals on," James smirked. "It's a door, not Moses' burning bush."

The doors opened half-way. A bent, twisted old man greeted them. He was sandwiched between two women wearing black hajibs, grey robes and white veils.

"Go away," snapped the old man. "We're full. There's no more room in the inn."

"Easy, father; it's me."

The old man poked his head out the door like a turtle from its shell. "Jeshua?"

"No, Abba... James."

One of the women took the old man's arm and led him away. The other woman invited them to enter a courtyard open to the sky. Females of various ages leaned over the balcony railings as they hung out wet laundry brought to them by soldiers from a nearby Roman military post. They vanished behind drapes of beaded ropes when they saw James and his companions.

The woman circled Rachel and said, "Welcome, the road to salvation leads here."

"Back off." James flipped his thumb at Lazarus. "She belongs to him."

She ignored James and said as she clasped Rachel's hand, "We are the sisters of redemption. We have come together under this roof to spread His love!"

A woman enveloped in a black chador rose from a fan-backed chair on the third floor. "That is enough, Atara!" She banged an ornately-carved cane on the rail of the balcony. From her throne, the mistress of the house was able to keep track of everything.

James herded Lazarus and Rachel to the stairs. On their way up they passed a trio of women scrubbing the floor on their hands and knees.

Mary advanced toward Lazarus when they arrived on her floor. She reversed her grip on the cane, hooked its lion-headed handle behind his neck and pulled him toward her. She pressed her palm against his cheek. "So it's true." Her head trembled under the hood of her black chador. "Judas stopped by on his way to Capernaum. I chalked off his rambling to too much wine."

She lowered the cane and limped through a pink archway into a chamber behind her chair. Wooden statues of animals and humans

135

ranging in height from a few inches to several feet were lined up like soldiers along the purple walls. The old man sat on the floor carving a doll out of a block of wood. He held up the doll.

"Peter has been with him the longest," he said and went back to his carving.

"Remember what Moses said about graven images, Abba."

Rachel cried as she smothered Mary's feet with kisses. "I have touched the mother of our saviour."

Mary recoiled. "Not another one, get her out of here. I can barely feed the ones I have."

"Abba, show this young lady your other creations." James placed Rachel's hand in his father's and accompanied them out of the room.

"Rachel hasn't been the same since…" Lazarus' sentence trailed off into nothingness.

"I know," Mary intervened. "My husband hasn't been quite right since Jeshua announced his mission."

James overheard Mary's words when he returned. "Damn it, mother. Come out with it. My brother believes he is the Messiah."

"Jeshua is disturbed. It runs in the family. My husband's nephew thinks he's a prophet. He lives in the desert like a savage, surviving on insects."

"That's it, Mother. Blame it on Abba."

Mary rapped her cane on a chair. James sat down and sulked. "My son," she said quietly, "could never accept the fact that his father was just a carpenter who got lucky. Better that I should be visited by some angel who filled me with God's seed."

Rachel reentered the room with Joseph. "Oh, blessed Virgin!"

Mary sidled up to Rachel. "You're a pretty girl, too pretty to waste your life cleaning floors and washing pagans' laundry while you wait for my son to show up and bestow a blessing on you."

"Mother of our Lord, I pledge to remain chaste and obedient. I would gladly stay here and consecrate myself to serving your son."

Mary slid a finger under the veil of the chador to wipe away a tear. "What a shame. Jeshua had such a future. Just look at how the women flock to him. If only those strange ideas had not taken hold of him, I could have been a grandmother by now."

When the sound of men's voices giving thanks drifted through a bow-shaped doorway, Mary hobbled onto the veranda. Below the balcony, Atara was passing out bread, cheese and milk to some lepers from the village. "Quit giving away our food," Mary screamed. "We don't have enough for ourselves without you feeding every beggar who comes by." Her body shuddered under the chador. "If I didn't watch them, we'd all starve."

"I need to find your son," Lazarus said.

"Everyone has a question for my son. I've heard them all. Can Jew and gentile eat together? Is it easier for a rich man or a poor man to enter the kingdom of heaven? Just how did he feed four thousand with a seven loaves of bread and a few fish?" Mary paused when the trio of scrub women fell on all fours in front of the open archway and went to work on the already immaculate floor. "I would like to know the answer to that last question myself," she said.

"Where is Jeshua?"

Mary retreated from Lazarus' frigid breath. "He has not returned since he deserted us three years ago."

"I need his help."

"Then you got a big problem," James interjected. "My brother isn't concerned with the real world. He lives to fulfil a prophecy."

"I have to find him. He has to help me." Lazarus looked out the window at the sun melting below the horizon. A few lepers moved secretively along Nazareth's outside walls on their way to the hostel. "Can't anyone answer my question?"

"There is only one answer that counts." James's voice grew thin and raspy. "My brother has to be brought back where he belongs before he gets into deep trouble."

"His blood is the wine which flows through your veins. His body is the staff of your body," Mary lamented.

"Blood, wine, body, bread!" James seized her words and flung them back at her. "I intend to save him, not eat him, Mother."

Rachel dashed onto the balcony. The lepers who had arrived from the village fled when she extolled, "Take, eat. This is His body. Take, drink. This is His blood. Do this in remembrance of Him."

"You have found out as much as you can here," James said as he led Rachel back into the room. "I'll find a place for you tonight."

"I won't have them here. I need all my beds. Four women are sleeping to a pallet as it is."

"Don't worry about it, Mother. They can stay at my place."

"You mean your whore's place." Mary wagged her finger at James. "If you wanted a good woman you had the pick of the litter here. But, no, my girls aren't good enough for you."

"I'm following in Jeshua's footsteps, Mother." James patted Lazarus on the back. "Let's get going. If I know Barabbas, he's stuffed my entire house into his pack by now."

As they trudged back to town, Lazarus looked over his shoulder. He saw the black-cloaked Madonna framed in the window like a harbinger of the judgement day to come.

It was dark when they arrived at James' house. Barabbas met them at the door. His arm was around Nidavah whose gown was unlaced from her neck to her navel. James brushed past them without speaking.

"Calm down. I left some silver on the table," Barabbas said.

"If you're finished here we'll leave in the morning." James stooped over a carpenter's tool chest. "I traded a Gaul two nights with Nidavah in exchange for these," he grunted as he opened the lid and took out a battle-axe. The bronze head of the axe was attached to a massive oak shaft. He reached into the chest again, removing a knee-length leather vest covered with circles of tin.

"You know we're headed in the same direction," James told Lazarus as he slipped the vest over his head. "Eventually all Messiahs end up in Jerusalem."

# 18

Rachel fell behind Barabbas and Lazarus on several occasions. Without success, Lazarus implored her to keep up with them. To avoid calling attention to a group of armed men travelling in the open, James had agreed to lead the Zealots through the wilderness, leaving the cobble road to the bandit leader and his tentative friends.

A man on a donkey rode by Barabbas. He dismounted, stepped off the path, turned his back and urinated.

"Stinking Samaritan, I'd like to cut him from ear to ear." Barabbas' remark was met by the sharp sting of a riding crop across his back. The bandit reeled around and found himself looking up at a Roman officer on horseback. Lazarus dropped his head. Hiding his face in the front of his robe, he joined the Samaritan at the side of the road.

The officer bumped his horse against Barabbas. "We decide who is allowed to travel our roads." Behind the officer were three foot-soldiers guarding a man chained by his feet and hands.

"Forgive me, sir." Barabbas cowered before the Roman. "I don't trust these Samaritans." He shuffled to the side of the horse, cupped his hand around his mouth and whispered, "They can't be trusted to keep the peace you have brought us."

The Roman jutted out his chin, wallowing in Barabbas' show of subservience. "Rome has a way of dealing with troublemakers," he said. Pulling on the reins of his horse, he turned its head toward the prisoner.

The prisoner's eyes were swollen shut. His features had melded under a glut of bruises. Through his broken jaw he managed to say, "Go to hell."

Lazarus raised his eye. He knew the voice of his rescuer from Revivim. Rachel started toward Bartholomew but halted when he croaked, "Get that whore away from me!" Lazarus bolted from the side of the Samaritan and hauled Rachel to the edge of the road. He held her wrist tightly to prevent her from going to the aid of Bartholomew.

"This is what happens to trash who defy Rome." The officer kicked Bartholomew in the face, sending him sprawling onto the stone surface of the road.

Barabbas raced over to Lazarus. "I despise these Zealots. They make a hard life even harder for honest men like ourselves." He ripped off the cloth covering Lazarus' face. "Zealots did this to him. They tortured him because they said he was too friendly with your people."

"This is one rebel who won't plague you anymore," the officer promised.

With the Roman's attention diverted, the Samaritan brought over a goatskin to the prisoner. He poured a trickle of water through Bartholomew's crushed lips.

"What do you think you're doing?" the officer asked.

"I am showing kindness to a stranger." The Samaritan continued ministering to Bartholomew.

"I thought your sect hated Jews."

"Their creed may not be ours, but we are all children of the same God."

"You're wasting your time, but do what you want. It's your water." The officer waved his men away. "Tiberius has ordered Herod and Pilate to adorn Jerusalem with the rotting corpses of these rebels during Passover."

Barabbas rubbed his hands together. "Excellent, that'll show the other trouble-makers."

"We caught this one," the Roman said, encouraging his horse to kick at Bartholomew, "because one of your people, a tavern-keeper in

Capernaum, betrayed him." As an afterthought he added, "No Roman would sell out his comrades."

"Ah, we're a weak people," Barabbas acknowledged.

"Nothing is truer than that. It's the fault of your religion. For instance, when I was in Galilee I listened to a priest, or whatever you call him, preaching to a multitude of fools. Turn your cheek; love your neighbour as you love yourself. What garbage. Yet they hung on his every word as though he were spewing gold." The Roman stiffened his legs and stood up in his stirrups. "We rule the world because the only god we worship is Rome. We leave loving one's enemies to the people we've conquered."

The officer motioned with his riding crop for the soldiers to jerk Bartholomew to his feet. "If I were you, I'd try to make it to Capernaum before nightfall. There is no telling what kind of scum you're liable to come across out here. In fact, once I drop this rebel off, I'm heading into the wilderness to track down one of our own, a deserter who killed the quartermaster and made off with the payroll."

The encounter with the officer unnerved Barabbas. He did not want to run the risk of confronting a Roman tracking party hunting for the rebels responsible for the massacre of the slave caravan. They left the highway and trekked across the desert in a straight line. When Barabbas felt confident they could no longer be seen from the road they veered south.

"This detour shouldn't cost us too much time," Lazarus told Rachel.

"Get serious," Barabbas snorted. "As fast as your woman is walking, it'll take us two days just to catch up with James."

"I won't slow you down." Rachel exaggerated the length of her stride, matching Barabbas footstep for footstep. She was determined not to provide the bandit with an excuse to abandon her along the road to Capernaum. "My faith in the chosen one will speed me toward Him. Even now I can hear Him summoning me."

Lazarus hollered after her, "Exhausting yourself is not going to get you there any sooner."

Rachel strove even harder to increase the distance between herself and Barabbas. Her advance was halted when she tripped over her own feet.

"Darling, we all have to accept our limitations," the bandit taunted, jogging by her. She massaged her twisted ankle with one hand while she searched the ground with the other one. She picked up a stone and threw it, missing Barabbas by more than six feet.

"If you can't aim any better than that, maybe you should go back to Mary."

Rachel gritted her teeth as she forced herself to put pressure on her swollen foot. She stumbled onward, trying to overtake Barabbas. Lazarus ran over, lifted her off her feet and carried her in the hammock formed out of his arms.

"Put me down," she said. But her plea was half-hearted. Lazarus' steady, unhurried gait began to lull her to sleep. "Barabbas will say I'm slowing us down and leave me." She buried her face into the front of his robe and dozed off. Lazarus sniffed her hair, closed his eyes and listened to her throaty breathing.

"Hello, I came back to see what was keeping you," Barabbas said and smirked. "I'm disappointed. I thought if your angel got tired, she could just whistle for Elijah to give her a lift in his fiery chariot. Sad to say, my very faith in miracles has been compromised."

James was piling stones onto a freshly dug grave when they caught up with the Zealots.

"What's going on?" Barabbas asked.

"He spoiled our fun." Elon pouted. "A Roman deserter wandered into our camp. We had to do something to kill time while we were waiting for you and decided —"

"They were butchering him like an animal." James backhanded Elon, preventing him from opening his mouth again. "I killed him and made them bury him."

"The boys got to do something to relieve the monotony." Barabbas looked at the stones stacked on the grave. He picked a rock and flipped it behind him. "Dig him up him; leave him for the jackals." His men scrambled for the mound.

James rushed forward to stop them. "The law says no corpse, including a stranger's, is to be left unburied."

"Okay, leave him buried, but get rid of the stones." Barabbas stamped on the mound, tamping it flat. "I don't need anyone coming along wanting to know who's under that pile."

Lazarus reluctantly agreed with Barabbas, "It's better not to call attention to the grave."

James walked to the mound and dropped a large stone at the head of the grave.

"I thought I made myself clear. I don't want this spot to be marked."

James shrugged as he sat down on the rock.

Barabbas trampled the grave and squatted in front of James. He dug his fingers into James' thigh.

James tightened the muscles in his leg. "My brother once tried to baptise me." James spoke in deliberate chopped sentences. "He is a great deal stronger than either of us."

"Your point being?"

"He failed. I never grovelled before him."

Barabbas released his grip. "We've rested long enough."

# 19

Lazarus instinctively covered his face when he passed through Capernaum's gates. James and Barabbas had convinced him that Rachel should remain on the outskirts of the village with the bandit's men to guard the weapons. They feared she might launch into an impromptu sermon in the Roman garrison town.

A guttural curse was directed at Lazarus when he bumped into someone. He pivoted on his heel. A blue-eyed Goliath with skin as pale and pitted as cheese curds dwarfed him. The giant's teeth had been filed into wolf-like fangs. His blond beard hung in tight braids past his waist. Each braid was threaded through a hand-carved ivory skull. James braced his hand in the middle of Lazarus' back and propelled him down the street.

Barabbas hurried to overtake Lazarus and James. His body went limp when he saw the giant joined by six other men wearing bearskin cloaks and leather breeches. Each man carried a bronze battle-axe and a quiver of throwing spears. They spoke in a language that resembled the barking of wild dogs.

"Gauls." Barabbas' voice was strained.

James chewed his thumbnail as he tracked the foreigners out of the corner of one eye. "They're not supposed to be this far south."

"What are Gauls?" Lazarus asked.

"Mercenaries. The Romans use them to guard the borders of their empire. They have only one notable talent. They are extremely efficient at killing."

Capernaum had flourished under the Roman occupation. The market square and the shops along its streets were packed with sellers and buyers. Yet as prosperous as the citizens of the town appeared to be, they went through the motions of their lives with little joy. Merchants sold their goods wearing blank expressions to equally vacuous customers. The clamour and haggling characteristic of other village market squares was absent. Commodities were bargained over in hushed tones. Only the clinking of silver on money trays indicated that any sort of commerce was taking place.

A vendor, exhibiting a basket of plump figs, appeared on the verge of tears when a centurion marched to his stall. The merchant shrank into the booth. His hands quivered. He held out a fig. The Roman did not take the fruit and nodded at the basket. With a timorous grin the vendor gave over the entire contents of the basket to the soldier, who swaggered off with the figs.

"Don't gawk." Barabbas steered Lazarus away from the fruit stall. "At least here, it's the Romans who terrorize us. In Jerusalem, it's our own people."

Barabbas and Lazarus fell behind James, allowing him to pilot them through the town and into a tavern. The building was packed with Roman soldiers in varying degrees of intoxication. Tiny bells and copper bangles tinkled as belly dancers performed on top of small tables placed throughout the tavern. The women expertly avoided the hands reaching out to fondle them, displaying more flesh than talent to the sex-starved soldiers.

James walked to the rear of the tavern and held open a curtain made of sea-shells for his companions. Inside an alcove Judas and Simon sat with two other men around a brass table. Judas rose partially to acknowledge Lazarus. Simon remained seated. A white-haired man, his back to the curtain, pored over a scroll. The man rolled up the vellum. He looked up at Lazarus and patted the cushion next to him.

"How fares your mother?"

Lazarus was momentarily taken aback by the presence of Lord Gamaliel in the squalid tavern. "Dead."

"And your wife?"

"Still mad."

"May her affliction serve Adonai's purpose." The priest lifted his eyes to the ceiling. "May the wisdom of Solomon guide our steps in these turbulent times."

"Is this the same wisdom which moved Saul to banish me from my village?"

"Saul!" Gamaliel spit out the name. "His kind are our true adversaries, not the Romans. Jews by birth only. They devote all their energies to maintaining their positions of comfort and wealth while scorning our traditions and laws."

Barabbas overcame his inclination to fall prostrate himself before the leader of the Sanhedrin, a man many regarded as a living saint. "I am Barabbas, your faithful servant."

"I know who you are. I know what you are." Gamaliel turned to James. "This is the second time I have seen the result of your brother's work." He peered into Lazarus' one good eye, studying him with scholarly detachment. "In there, behind the darkness of the pupil burns a light. It is his soul." He paused, unrolled the scroll again, and ran his finger down the parchment, shaking his head as he read to himself. He placed his hands on both sides of Lazarus' head and proclaimed, "Demons do not have souls."

Barabbas, smarting from the slight paid him by Gamaliel, bent over. His nose came within an inch of touching the priest's nose. "If it's a peep show you want, old man, go out there. The women are doing everything but fucking the soldiers under your self-righteous snout."

A square-jawed ox of a man, who up until now had remained sullen and dumb, slammed his fist on the table. Barabbas leapt to his feet. Simon and Judas forced Barabbas' arms behind his back in a hammer-lock and wrestled him to his knees.

The ox pinched Barabbas' ear and pulled him toward him. "I get my best intelligence reports from those girls. They're like the daughters of Esther to our rebellion."

146

"Sorry, I didn't catch your name." Barabbas grimaced as the man pulled harder. "If you insist on ripping my ear off, I may never hear it."

"Peter, one of Jeshua's followers, or at least I was, until he strayed from the cause." The man released Barabbas.

"My heart goes out to the young preacher," Gamaliel sighed.

"It's becoming impossible to go anywhere these days without hearing about Jeshua." Barabbas rapped his knuckles on the table restlessly.

Peter's eye twitched. He spoke through one side of his down-turned mouth. "Why are you here?"

James rushed in with an answer. " Herod and Pilate are..."

"I'm talking to this thief," the fisherman growled.

Barabbas pushed himself away from the table. His neck muscles grew tense as he prepared to spring at anyone who approached him.

"Behave yourself." Peter wagged his finger as if scolding a truculent child. "One word from me and those soldiers out there will mince you into bits too small to feed a cat. Romans are by and large very loyal. You see, they believe that I'm their friend."

Barabbas dipped into his purse. He scattered a fistful of coins on the table. "We took these from a Roman slave patrol. I think they are to be used to pay fresh troops."

Peter shrugged. "New soldiers arrive all the time."

"That's what I thought until I found out that Tiberius intends to turn Jerusalem into a slaughter yard during Passover. I believe part of the money is to pay for the round-up of rebels."

"Old news." Peter yawned. "We knew about this two weeks ago. The Sadducees convinced Pilate that Rome should intensify its drive to eradicate any sect or figure who represents a threat to its authority. Zealots, Essenes, Pharisees, anyone who has made life difficult for Herod and his friends was targeted."

Gamaliel interjected, "I sent one of the high priests to Herod to dissuade him from putting Tiberius' plans into action. In exchange for his intervention Caiaphas promised Herod that we will give him the leaders of the rebellion, including Jeshua."

"I'm to turn over the master." Judas held up a single coin. "Caiaphas was so grateful to me that he convinced the council of elders to give me thirty pieces of silver when the job is done."

"Jeshua's not a Zealot," Lazarus stammered.

"I know that." Peter rose to his feet. "While the council is occupied conducting its trial, we'll be sowing the seeds of the rebellion. The infidels will be driven from David's city."

Peter placed his hand on Barabbas' forearm. "I hear you're angry that our leaders have not requested for you to join us."

"Not so much angered as dazed by our leaders' stupidity," Barabbas replied.

"We need you and your men."

Barabbas arched his eyebrows. "And where do we fit into your plans?" he asked suspiciously.

"For the uprising to be a success we need a diversion. You're to attack Nicopolis to draw most of the Roman garrison from Jerusalem. It's far away enough that the troops will be unable to return in time to reinforce what is left of Pilate's soldiers."

"I'd rather be in Jerusalem in the midst of the fighting," Barabbas said. "This is where my men can be put to best use."

Peter shook his head. "Your people lack discipline."

"Friend, when it comes to the crunch discipline doesn't mean squat. The Romans have crushed the best-trained, best-disciplined armies on earth. The only people they have failed to subjugate are those nations who refuse to fight them by the book."

The ancient patriarch wrung his hands as he refuted Barabbas' words. "It is our laws that distinguish us from the beasts."

"The Torah is not going to defeat Tiberius," Barabbas derided Gamaliel.

"We live by those laws!" Gamaliel roared.

"The only way to defeat the Romans is to be like Joshua, become merciless, abandon all vestiges of pity and compassion."

Lazarus had sat in silence as the details of the plot were revealed. "Is this the future of our people?" He swept his hand toward Judas, Simon, and Peter. "I have reason to hate Jeshua, but even I am sickened by your treachery." His body shook violently.

"Judge not lest you be judged." Peter's presence filled the room. "Jeshua is well aware of his role on earth."

James nodded. "He's right. My brother's entire life has been dedicated to fulfilling Isaiah's prophecy."

"Jeshua will arrive in Jerusalem on Sunday. He sent Simon and me ahead of him to prepare for his entrance into the city," Judas said.

"Let me talk to Lazarus alone." Gamaliel gestured with a feeble flick of his hand for the others to leave. When they had vacated the alcove Gamaliel asked, "Do you love Israel?"

"Look at my face. I'm beyond either love or hate."

Unfazed by Lazarus' expression of self-contempt, Gamaliel continued, "Jeshua is determined to die. Regardless of how quick we are in mounting our attack, he will condemn himself by his own passion before we can save him." Gamaliel picked up the scroll and spread it on the table. He pointed at the words. "Read."

"I can't. I don't know how." Lazarus' admission of ignorance shamed him.

"Elijah brought back the widow's son from death; his student restored the son of the Shunammite." Gamaliel rolled up the scroll. "Yet when it was their own time, they could not resist the hand of God and died."

"This means nothing to me. All I want is to be freed from this hideous body and have my wife restored to me."

"I spared your life once." Gamaliel tied a yellow piece of ribbon around the scroll and thrust it into Lazarus' hand. "Now I am asking you to help me save another."

"I don't understand."

"When the time comes you will know what to do." Gamaliel placed his hand on Lazarus' head, as though delivering a benediction. "To save a hand sometimes one must cut off a finger."

# 20

Gamaliel left Lazarus alone in the alcove to ponder the riddle, "To save a hand…" Racking his brain, Lazarus turned the phrase inside-out, struggling to decipher the priest's message. Useless. It was an exercise designed for students of Torah, not for an illiterate labourer who recited the Shema from memory.

Gamaliel and the others were gone when Lazarus finally staggered through the curtain of shells. He looked around the room of soldiers ogling women who had sacrificed their virtue for Israel. Gasps and feigned retching noises prompted Lazarus to feel for the cloth covering his face. It was no longer there. He panicked and plowed through a group of soldiers at the front of the tavern watching a dancer make love to an invisible suitor. The irate soldiers grappled with Lazarus and pitched him through the door. He tumbled into the street, bowling over a man in his path, and landed face down in the dirt.

Lazarus tried to get up but was pinned to the earth by a fur-covered boot grinding into his spine.

"Once is an accident, twice is a mistake." The stench of rancid beer washed over Lazarus as his assailant struggled in Aramaic to make his displeasure heard as well as felt. "Three times never happens."

A hand the breadth of a shovel cuffed Lazarus across the side of his head. Using all the muscles in his legs and arms, he catapulted the boot's owner into the air.

Crouched on all fours, Lazarus and the Gaul he had collided with earlier took one another's measure. The hatred on the blond giant's face was chilling. Lazarus lowered his head and charged the giant like a ram, knocking him on his backside. Then he sprang to his feet and raced off in search of James and Barabbas before his newly-acquired enemy could recover.

Lazarus dashed through Capernaum's gate. He ignored a sentry's order for him to stand to be checked. There was no one to be found when he arrived at the place where he had left Rachel. He shielded his eyes with the side of his hand and peered out into the countryside.

The sun bouncing off a metal object impelled Lazarus to pursue the flashes of light until he climbed a hill and came across Barabbas and James. The Zealots, concealed behind a clump of scraggly trees, watched a caravan consisting of six wagons. The train was escorted by eleven of Herod's palace guards and two Roman centurions on horseback.

"Where is Rachel?" Lazarus demanded.

"She went with Peter." Barabbas eyed the caravan greedily.

James paced back and forth, slapping his hand against his thigh. "If we had any sense we would be on our way too."

Lazarus shook Barabbas by his shoulders. "Why didn't you stop her?"

"Stop her! She was so keen to meet her master that she would have castrated anyone who stood in her way." Barabbas wrenched himself free. "Relax. You'll see her in Jerusalem."

"Provided we don't get killed before then," James said.

"I need to get a better look." Barabbas crawled a hundred yards down the hill on his belly for a closer inspection of the caravan. At the front of the train was a gilded sedan borne by four Ethiopians. The silhouettes of two women could be seen through the cab's gossamer-like window coverings. Mounted centurions in full battle regalia rode next to the sedan. The wind blew back the drapes enclosing the cab; sunlight penetrated its interior and bounced off a silver dome balanced on one of the occupants' laps.

"Psst," Barabbas hissed. "The coins in those wagons are calling me."

"We can't afford to jeopardize our plans," James grumbled.

"You mean the plan where me and my men get killed fending off the entire Jerusalem garrison while your friends make like heroes?"

"If you had a problem with this, why didn't you back out in Capernaum?"

"I'm not backing out, I'll be there when you need me. But for right now I want what's in that caravan. At nightfall we'll attack, take everything — gold, horses, women, their lives — everything."

At sunset the bearers halted, carefully putting down the sedan before collapsing in exhaustion. The guards pitched camp. Barabbas noted where the sentries were stationed to determine the best spot to enter the bivouac unseen. The slaughter would not last long. After the wagons had been looted he would give the women to his men. They deserved a little entertainment, considering what awaited them in Nicopolis. The elite troops of the Jerusalem garrison could be held at bay only temporarily. More than likely, all of his men would be annihilated.

The bandit continued to scrutinise the caravan while Lazarus stared at the night sky. The moon, ensnared in a mesh of stars, shone brightly against the onyx backdrop of the heavens. He turned to Barabbas but the bandit was gone.

Barabbas walked up to his men, who were gathered in counsel at the top of the ridge. He stepped into the middle of their discussion. His presence was met by belligerent protests. He selected the loudest of the dissenters and knocked him down, daring the man to follow him or fight him.

James joined Lazarus. He threw his thumb backward in the direction of the bandit. "Sounds like Barabbas has a mutiny on his hands."

Lazarus closed his eyes. He propped his elbows on his knees, resting his chin on his palms. "Imagine the nation they'll create."

Abruptly the chorus of angry voices ceased. A half-hearted murmur of consent filled the air. Lazarus opened his good eye. Barabbas came toward him carrying a pack roll. He stopped and looked at the sky.

"Vultures. That's odd, I've never seen them at night." Several of the scavenger birds circled the wagons.

"Maybe they know something we don't," James said.

"Like what?"

"Like risking everything to attack that caravan is stupid."

"I don't believe in omens." Barabbas unrolled his pack. He removed his breastplate and greaves. "Nor do my men."

"From the sound of your quarrel with them, maybe you're wrong about that," Lazarus said.

"Quarrel? That was no quarrel. It was a minor disagreement. All I had to do was make them see things my way. I promised them two things. Number one, whatever they take is theirs alone." Barabbas strapped on his greaves. "The second promise, the one that I think put them on my side, dealt with you. I pledged to let them kill you if you refuse to join us."

"I'm not going."

"That goes for me, too," James said. "I won't participate in something that endangers the plan."

"Lost your nerve, eh? I guess the taste of blood offends your delicate sensibilities."

Lazarus drew the sword Barabbas had given him. "Enough!" He snapped the blade of the weapon across his knee.

Barabbas clicked his tongue against the roof of his mouth. "Don't be so negative." He glanced at the sky. "Now, there's an omen I can trust." A thick formation of clouds drifted over the moon. The desert was shrouded in blackness. "What they can't see can't hurt us."

The Zealots spread out over the terrain to take up their attack positions. It was Barabbas' task to eliminate the sentries by slashing their throats so deftly that not even a whimper would escape their lips. He would whistle twice when he had completed his task. On the second blast of his whistle his men were to swoop down on the camp. Although they would save the women till last, they would spare no one, for no enemy of the Lord should expect or receive mercy. Was it not Adonai who commanded Joshua to burn the great cities of Canaan, pillage its wealth, rape its women, and slay every denizen from the eldest matriarchs to the infants suckling at their mothers' breasts, so that the land promised to Moses would be delivered into the hands of Israel?

Barabbas dispatched the sentries in less than fifteen minutes. A guard lay on his stomach at the bandit's feet. Blood oozed from the gash across his neck, encircling his head like a halo. Barabbas wet his lips. He formed a fork out of his first two fingers, inserted them into his mouth and blew with such force that his whistle shattered the stillness of the night.

The small band of rebels charged down the hill. "Shield of Joshua, save and guard us. Blessed be the Lord!" The battle cry rose from the depth of their beings as they rushed to do God's will.

Barabbas waited for his men to reach the base of the hill, then led the assault. Four guards, seeing Barabbas enter the camp, rushed him with their lances held out in front of them. He slashed at them with his sword, cutting through their midst as a reaper would through a field of wheat. Herod's men lacked the resolve to challenge him further and fled. The Zealots ran them down, butchering them despite their appeals for clemency. As Barabbas veered off in the direction of the sedan, the centurions vaulted into their saddles and galloped toward the wagons.

Barabbas ripped down the drape covering the cabin's door. He extended his hand graciously to its occupants. The women shrank from his touch and embraced one another. He seized the older of the two women by her wrist, a dark-skinned lady wearing her abundant black hair piled on top of her head. She extracted a long ivory pin from her hair, plunging it into Barabbas' left eye. His wail of agony was drowned out by the sound of confusion and terror coming from his men.

He whirled around, covering his maimed eye with his hand. A river of blood surged through the cracks between his fingers. With only one eye left to him, Barabbas was barely able to see the centurions pull their horses up to the wagons and slice the ropes securing the canopies to their frames. The canvases flew off. From the interior of the wagons a company of Roman soldiers and Gauls stormed the Zealots.

Barabbas, momentarily paralysed, reclaimed his valour and madly dashed to the aid of his men. He had not gone more than fifty feet when a centurion struck him with the flat of his sword blade.

Flight was futile. These were not common foot soldiers the Zealots were facing. These were men who had cut their teeth on battlefields from Greece to the mountains of Sicily, the elite of Tiberius' strike force, whose sole purpose was to exterminate rebels throughout the empire.

The Romans and their mercenaries formed a ring around Barabbas' men. Every time the Zealots tried to breach the circle the loop would tighten. The last six rebels left standing were forced to their knees. Barabbas emerged from his stupor in time to witness the Gauls drop coarse hemp garrottes over his men's heads and slowly strangle them. He tried to stand but was booted in the stomach by the centurion who had struck him. The Roman jerked Barabbas' head back by his hair. Breathing heavily in the bandit's face, he held Barabbas still as a Gaul plodded toward them with a rope drenched in the blood of his previous victim.

Barabbas gagged on his tongue. The garrotte cut into his throat. Brilliant flashes of light appeared before him. He tightened his neck muscles. As he drifted between life and death he heard a woman's voice.

"Stop! We'll bring this one to Jerusalem."

The centurion pushed away the Gaul. The tension in Barabbas' neck muscles gradually loosened. He gasped for air.

The woman glided toward the Roman carrying a domed tray. "Don't be so glum, Lysias. Your plan to use us as a decoy succeeded."

Lysias frowned. "I won't be satisfied until I've slain the one who left me alive in Revivim."

The woman lifted the dome of the tray. "What better way to redeem your honour and show your gratitude for assuming the command of the Jerusalem garrison than to present two gifts to Pilate?" The stern visage of John the Baptist, his mouth agape as though still railing against his foes, stared sightless from the surface of the platter. "The head of a renegade and the body of a rebel."

Behind the woman appeared a young girl dressed in a transparent silk gown. She pranced through the camp, bending over the corpses of Barabbas' men, and shimmied her breasts before their dead faces. "Mother, see how they smile. They are so much friendlier in death." She looked up to the hills, but failed to see Lazarus slip behind the cover of the rock from where he had witnessed the slaughter.

# 21

James and Lazarus found a cave to hide in while Lysias' men combed the hills for any rebels who might have escaped. After three days had passed, they left the cave and walked among their dead.

Flies rose like Job's whirlwind when Lazarus gathered up the bodies. He dug a common grave with a Roman shield. The elements and scavengers had desecrated the rebels' corpses beyond recognition. Digging was slow work. He came to the startling realisation that the pursuit of Jeshua was irrevocably driving his people toward oblivion. All the miracles Jeshua had wrought were actually a sentence of death.

Lazarus sprinkled a handful of earth over the burial mound. James recited the Mourner's Kaddish for his countrymen without emotion, believing that it was their lack of commitment to the sacred cause which had brought the wrath of God upon them.

"Jeshua will have arrived in Jerusalem by now. If it hadn't been for Barabbas we could have greeted him as he entered the city," James said as he built a cairn of stones to mark the grave of these imperfect heroes. He placed the last stone on the pillar of rocks and started off after Lazarus.

Lazarus did not slow down when James called him. James mustered a burst of energy and caught up with him. "We'll have to travel all day and night if we're to get there in time for the seder."

Lazarus gazed at the broken set of mountains rising from the plains. "Then we better keep walking." Shortly they would cross valleys of

Kidron and Hinnom and see the great hill upon which David had built his capital.

"Without Barabbas how are we going to create a diversion?"

"Perhaps we are the diversion," Lazarus answered.

By Wednesday morning they came within sight of Jerusalem's massive, bleached outer walls. Standing over forty feet high and manned by a combined force of Pilate's and Herod's elite soldiers, the ramparts served as the first line of defence against attack. Behind the main fortifications, a smaller set of walls encased the ancient city, which had spread well beyond its original boundaries, spilling down the eastern and western slopes of the mountains.

David had chosen the rugged hilltop as the site of his capital for its seeming invulnerability to assault from enemies existing within Judea. It was written that King Saul slew the priests of Shilo, but it was David who stole the word of God and conveyed it to what would become the heart of the kingdom he would forge. Two nations of Jews melded by force of arms, held together by one man's will, could not long survive beyond him.

It was neither the Greeks nor the Romans who conquered the land. Israel itself was to blame for its demise as a nation. Solomon, despite his much-vaunted wisdom for resolving conflicts by threatening to cleave babies in half, could not stop his own sons from rending the kingdom like a cheap garment. It was whispered by some of the more radical messianic sects that Jerusalem itself was cursed, that David's commandeering of the tabernacle and transporting it to his capital was a desecration. His son had magnified the sacrilege by imprisoning the spirit of a deity born and nurtured in the wilderness inside a glorious tomb. The mystics argued that the existence of Jerusalem was a cancer that had to be removed before the anointed one would reveal himself and create Eden on earth once more.

Though only a mile or two from the city, James refused to go further. He dropped to his knees, touched the ground with his forehead, and began chanting a prayer of thanks.

"Get up." Lazarus was irritated by his companion's display of religious devotion.

"Tomorrow is Pesach. We have to fast." James was firm in his refusal to go on. "We can't enter the city until tomorrow."

Lazarus rose before James. He unrolled his pack and assembled a clean wardrobe. He slipped a white gown over his head. On top of his robe he donned a rough chestnut-coloured coat with sleeves made of camel hair. It took him numerous tries to properly dress his head in a large scarlet kerchief in the style of the Bedouin. He wound a twisted cord around his forehead to hold the koufyeh in place and wrapped the fabric hanging down around his face.

His identity was safe. He was no longer Lazarus the Jew, no longer the crude manifestation of Jeshua's divinity. Dressed as a Bedouin, he could walk the streets without fear of attracting the attention of either the Romans or worse, Jeshua's followers. When the time was right, he would reveal himself to the only one who mattered.

James tossed in his sleep under a thin blanket. Lazarus nudged him with his foot. James shook off his sleep and sat up. Lazarus passed him a hard chunk of bread.

"I had a strange dream. Corpses, millions of them, were marching in place in front of a long red building, their gaunt faces fixed on my brother. They stretched out their arms as though petitioning him for mercy. He turned his back on them as they entered the building."

"Eat." Lazarus handed another crust of bread to James. "Fasting brings on weird dreams."

James reached under his bedding, pulled out a water sack and soaked the dried bread to soften it enough to chew. "This will have to hold us until tonight," he said. "We won't be able to get much in the way of food in the city today."

By noon they arrived at the main gates. All other entrances into the city had been closed to maintain security during the feast of Pesach. A line of more than a hundred people had formed in front of the iron-clad wooden portals. Roman soldiers patted down each person who had made the pilgrimage to Jerusalem and opened their bags.

After having cleared the first inspection, the people were subjected to another search at the gate of the inner walls by Herod's guards.

Herod's palace, one of many constructed throughout the land with the surplus of taxes he extorted from his people, cast its shadow over the streets. The palace was protected from attack by the proximity of the fortress of Antonio. The formidable stone citadel attested that Jerusalem was Rome's property.

The narrow road leading up to a steep flight of stairs, just wide enough to provide a place to set one's feet, was littered with trampled palm leaves. Throngs of people were moving from one stratum of the city to the next. From each landing of the central flight of stairs countless dark streets extended, creating a labyrinth of corridors that comprised the residential quarters of Jerusalem.

Before reaching the last level, which yawned into the expansive plaza of the Temple Mount, they paused to listen to one of the hundreds of self-proclaimed prophets who preached messages of doom and judgement throughout the city.

"Repent, for the coming of the Messiah is at hand." The oracle, dressed in sackcloth and smeared from head to toe in ashes, proclaimed from a platform. He scampered down from his pulpit, racing toward a Sadducee escorted by two burly Roman centurions. The soldiers carried standards with the likeness of Tiberius stamped on the disks attached to their staffs. The oracle veered away from the Sadducee and flung himself on a soldier. He grappled with the centurion for possession of the standard. Finally, wresting the pole from the Roman, he hurled it down the stairs.

"Idolaters, heathens, apostates, graven images are an abomination to God!" The prophet covered his head in anticipation of a beating.

"Hold your hand," the other soldier ordered his comrade when he raised his fist. "This fool's not worth causing an incident." He pushed the oracle to the side and continued down the stairs. With so many people in Jerusalem, the Romans took care to avoid any confrontation which could ignite a full-scale rebellion.

Tensions were already high enough in the city following the arrival, the preceding Sunday, of a young mystic who had been met by a large group of his followers. The mystic had immediately set out to insult the religious establishment, engaging them in heated discussions which called into question their vision of orthodoxy. The old order leaders of the community had tried to trap him into making statements for which he could be condemned for heresy if he sided with Rome, or sedition if he went against it. Annas, one of Herod's lackeys in the Sanhedrin, had gone so far as to ask the mystic if it was lawful to give tribute to Caesar. The Galilean was no fool. To condone the hated tax could result in his losing the devotion of many of his supporters; to condemn it openly would result in his being charged with sedition. The mystic gave a response which even the most wily senator in Rome would have been hard pressed to concoct.

"Whose image is on the coin?" he had asked. When told the coin was stamped with Tiberius' likeness he answered, "Then render unto Caesar the things that are Caesar's, and unto God the things that are God's." The mystic slipped into the mob that had come to hear the debate before Annas could frame another question.

The new garrison commander had sided with the Sanhedrin's request to arrest Jeshua and bring him before a religious council and civil court to explore his beliefs. Lysias had cautioned Pilate not to take the presence of the mystic lightly. "Clever men are more dangerous to the order of Rome than violent men."

Pilate agreed reluctantly after Lysias informed him of his own encounter with seemingly harmless Jews in Revivim. The experience had scarred the young captain. Secretly Lysias prayed that open rebellion would occur so that he could drench the land in the blood of Jews and destroy everything they held dear and sacred. A warrant was issued, but Jeshua had vanished.

James and Lazarus entered an open plaza. They stood near the foot of the marble stairs leading up to a poor replica of Solomon's temple. The pillars supporting the cypress and cedar roof of the sanctuary had long ceased to gleam white. Occupation by a host of conquerors along with centuries of neglect had taken their toll on the building. Gold and silver religious artifacts, censers, Menorahs, Torah crowns, the very leaf gilding the tabernacle, had been stripped and carted away so many times by foreigners that the priests had not bothered to replace them. Instead, they relied on tinselled imitations of the original artifacts in the execution of their sacred duties.

Hawkers plied their trade at the base of the Temple, selling everything from food and drink to scraps of parchment upon which were written a host of prayers calling for divine intervention in matters ranging from animal husbandry to love. People bumped and tripped each other as they clambered up the stairs to hand over their Pesach offerings. The Levites, the Temple's custodians, washed their hands in mock gold water basins each time they weighed an oblation and placed the offering in a wicker basket.

The procession lasted all day. At dusk a shofar sounded. A high priest, garbed in a tunic made of purple, blue and red wool and wearing a pair of white linen breeches, walked out of the Temple's inner sanctum. He took special care not to cross a black stripe painted on the floor of the outer sanctuary, a line defining the boundary between the worlds of God and man. Over the tunic the priest wore an ephod, a vest-like garment. Fastened to the ephod's shoulder straps were two silver bars with the names of the twelve sons of Jacob engraved on them.

The priest's gold breastplate, adorned with four rows of precious stones, dazzled the assembled people with its brilliance in the waning sunlight. The priest held aloft the disembowelled carcass of a freshly slaughtered lamb. He threw it into a fire that raged in a bronze pit. The worshippers swayed from side to side, chanting joyously, as they waited for the priest to lift his staff and pronounce a benediction so that they could go on their way to celebrate the seder, the commemoration of their flight from Egypt.

James and Lazarus remained in the plaza after most of the people had departed. Eventually the priest who had bestowed the blessing on the crowd re-emerged from the Temple without his ceremonial raiments. He crooked a finger at them, pulled the hood of his robe over his head and hurried down the stairs. They followed him around the side of the sanctuary. The priest halted, pointing at the red glow of torches and bonfires flickering between the inner and outer walls of the city at the bottom of the Temple Mount. He started to descend the steep bank. When they came to the base of the hill, they passed through an archway.

Sandwiched between the two walls on a narrow strip of land was the Shadow Jerusalem, a squalid, foul-smelling home to beggars, lepers, tax collectors and other social outcasts. It was a city of gambling dens, and of brothels catering to men who desired more than simple sex and who had the wealth to satisfy those desires. Within the flimsy buildings, constructed out of whatever material the inhabitants of the nether city could scrounge from the dung and refuse piles outside the main wall, sins only dreamt of during Manasseh's reign were realised. Children, eunuchs and old women begged passersby to enter into their dark hovels and share their lives for a hour or so. The Shadow Jerusalem was allowed to survive because it was believed to be better to acknowledge the existence of depravity and keep it interned between the walls than to risk the sickness spilling over into the holy city. Though the Roman and Jewish authorities periodically burned out the settlers for show, a new Shadowland would grow on the ruins of the old one and soon the dregs of society swarmed over it like maggots on a bloated corpse.

The priest hastened past the rubble and garbage strewn along the road. He guided James and Lazarus to a two-storey house. Unlike the other dwellings in the Shadowland, this one was made of quarried stone. A small courtyard enclosed by a brick wall was attached to the house. James pulled the priest aside, conferring with him for a moment. The priest nodded and brushed against Lazarus as he raced back toward the base of the Temple Mount.

James swung open the gate of the courtyard. He bent over to pluck a leaf from a plant growing in the garden patch behind the wall. He rubbed it between his palms, held his hands up to his nose and inhaled.

He extended his palms under Lazarus' nose. The scent of fresh mint filled Lazarus' nostrils, temporarily blocking out the stench of the Shadow Jerusalem.

Lazarus glanced around the courtyard. The house more than likely belonged to one of the Jewish publicans who, despite the wealth they were able to amass, were forbidden to live within the city proper. Because of their function as tax collectors and their daily intercourse with the Romans, they were regarded by decent Jerusalemites as pariahs, as vile and wretched as any of the sodomites plying their trade between the walls.

James lifted a heavy iron knocker. It crashed against the door of the house. A small portal slid open a crack. A bloodshot eye darted from side to side. The person on the other side grunted as he struggled to lift a large beam securing the door. Lazarus, growing impatient, braced his shoulder against the door and forced it open. He was met by a rotund man who, if standing on his tiptoes, would not have reached Lazarus' chin. The little man was smartly dressed. He wore a kaftan cut from the finest cloth and the latest in Western fashion, a covered shoe with a heel.

He bowed to James. "I am honoured to have you and your brother grace my house this feast of Pesach." He then addressed Lazarus, whose hulking form blocked the doorway. "Have you heard the gospel? Do you seek the truth?"

"We are all seekers of the truth, Matthew," James responded. "He is —"

Taking care to ensure his face was completely covered, Lazarus tapped James on the shoulder and shook his head. "He is my servant, my bodyguard," James finished his sentence.

Matthew smiled sadly. "Times are dangerous for men of vision and peace." His doleful expression vanished as suddenly as it had surfaced. From the back of the house, Rachel appeared carrying a decanter of pinkish liquid. James started to speak as she passed between them, sprinkling rose-scented water, but stopped.

"Where is my husband?" Rachel asked, looking at the Bedouin. "The Master is anxious to see him." Lazarus lowered his head so that she could not see his eyes.

James lied, "He has been detained. He will meet us later."

"Jeshua is pleased with this one." Matthew smiled at Rachel. "He has asked me to record her sayings. Her words capture his message in a language that everyone can understand." Rachel finished dousing James and Lazarus with the rose water. She dashed up a flight of stairs to the second floor and climbed a ladder leading to the roof.

"Follow her," Matthew instructed James. "Your brother has already started to read the Haggadah."

"Won't you be joining us at the seder table?" James asked.

"The words which fall from Jeshua's lips are nourishment enough for me. Your brother invited me to share the feast, but I know that though I am one of his most faithful students, there are those who resent my inclusion as a disciple."

What Matthew said was true. Even James found Jeshua's choice of company unsettling. In part it was his brother's acceptance of all people without reservation which had raised the ire of the Pharisees and Sadducees alike. He shared the same table, and some went so far as to hint, the same bed, with whores, publicans, lepers, and gentiles alike.

Rachel propped open the trap door. James and Lazarus scaled the ladder after her. A long table, sheltered from the elements by a thatched canopy, occupied the centre of the rooftop. Lazarus managed to remain inconspicuous by hiding in the shadow of a reed screen a few yards away from the table. Sitting on pillows were twelve men who leaned to the right on their elbows as they drained what was the first of four goblets of wine to be consumed this night. Rachel let the trap door slam shut and took her place behind Jeshua. The muscular red-haired champion of the gathering sat on a chair rather than on the roof's surface with his disciples.

"Why is this night different than any other night?" Jeshua asked. He gave the answer before anyone could reply. "Because men of peace are condemned and hunted." He drained his goblet and went on. "Because this night the head of a righteous man is paraded around Herod's palace on a pole."

Jeshua banged his empty wine goblet on the table. From behind the screen, Mary Magdalene emerged to fill his chalice until wine spilled over its rim. He licked the wine from his hand. "Here, drink," he slurred, passing the goblet to Judas, who sat on his left side. "Drink it… because?"

Rachel whispered in Jeshua's ear, "This is the blood of my testament, which is shed for mankind for the remission of their sins."

Jeshua's hands fluttered in the air as he beckoned Mary toward him. She placed a piece of unleavened bread in his hands. His chin dropped to his chest. "My burden is heavy." His green eyes became turquoise. He jumped to his feet, picked up his chair and flung it off the roof. "The spirit is willing, but the flesh is weak!" He swept his arm over the gathering as he stumbled to the trap door. "Watch and pray, that you avoid temptation."

Judas and Peter ran after him. Judas laid his hand on Jeshua's arm but was tossed aside as though he were a straw doll.

"Get away from me! The Son of Man goes where it is written He must: but there is no pity for the one who betrays the Son of Man. It would be better for that person if he had not been born."

"Master, are you saying I'm a traitor?"

Jeshua lifted the trap door. "From your mouth, not mine," he laughed without joy.

"You have no enemies here," Peter said, as Jeshua climbed down the ladder.

"This night before the cock crows, you will deny me three times." He dropped from the ladder, landing on his feet.

"I will not deny you even if I am threatened with death."

"Then follow me, watch over me. I need air, a place to pray."

Matthew held open the door for Jeshua, who paused briefly to kiss him on his cheek.

"You I love, because you want no more from me than that which I am." Jeshua lurched into the courtyard and wobbled down the road, closely followed by Peter and two new converts, the Zebedee brothers.

Lazarus went to the edge of the roof to watch them. They were headed in the direction of an olive grove planted on a small hill beyond the main walls of the city. Judas and James left the house next, proceeding in the opposite direction from their fellow disciples.

# 22

Jeshua gasped when he passed through the dung gate. He raced by the steaming mounds of garbage and excrement piled beyond the walls of the city. The scraggly olive grove, a vestige of the agricultural foundation of Jerusalem, clung tenaciously to the rocky soil of the hill. He succeeded in reaching the midpoint of the mount before Peter and the new converts caught up with him.

"What garden is this?" Jeshua whacked a stick against the trunk of a warped olive tree.

"It is Gethsemane, the same grove we visited when you first called us together," Peter answered.

"It is strange what springs from untended gardens." A smile crept across Jeshua's face. "This is where Mary Magdalene heeded my calling." He wandered through the stand of trees, banging his stick against their trunks until it broke in half. "You reap what you sow, eh?" Jeshua walked deeper into the grove until he came to a pool fed by an artesian spring. He looked over his shoulder at Peter. "My soul is exceeding sorrowful, even unto death: stay here and watch over me."

Peter and the Zebedee brothers sat on a boulder near the edge of the water. Peter handed Jeshua one of the three wine sacks he had taken with him from Matthew's house. Jeshua drained half the sack, dribbling the blood-red liquid down the bib of his robe. He wandered off from his companions, shaking his fist at them when they called after him.

"Leave me alone!" he demanded.

Unsteadily, Jeshua walked into the middle of the grove and tripped. He propped himself against a tree. "O my Father, if it be possible, let this cup pass from me." He turned the wine sack upside down, squeezing the last drops of juice from it. "Not as I will, but as you will." He stood and went back to the pond to find that Peter and his friends had fallen asleep. "What, could you not keep watch with me one hour?" he asked as he searched the area around the rock, discovering the other wine pouches that Peter had brought along with him.

Jeshua returned to the spot where he had fallen. He plopped on the ground, placed a sack on his lap, and lifted the spout of the other wine bag to his mouth. "O my Father, if this cup may not pass away from me, except I drink it, then your will be done."

"Amen," said a voice from within the tangle of trees.

Through the blur of his wine-induced stupor, Jeshua saw a figure with a head of red fire approaching. "Are you my angel of revelation?" he asked.

"What do you think?" Lazarus stepped out of the trees into the moonlight. He unwrapped his scarlet koufyeh and cocked his head so that the moon illuminated his features in its pale light.

"Oh, it's you," Jeshua snorted. He took another swig of wine. "Isn't one miracle in a lifetime enough?" He held up his thumb and lined up Lazarus as though he were an artist inspecting his work. "I have been given power over flesh."

Lazarus rolled his koufyeh in a ball and hurled it at Jeshua. "It would have been better if you had left me to rot in peace." The koufyeh unravelled in flight, floating harmlessly to the ground. "I came here for another one of your so-called acts of divinity. I came here for you to make right what you started."

Jeshua wiped his lips on his sleeve, staining the white fabric crimson. "That's too bad, because I confess I'm not an expert at restorative miracles. I brings 'em back as they are, not as they were." He tossed the other wine bag to Lazarus. "Drink for the remission of my sins."

"You abused your power. You've made me a thing of nightmares, a name spoken by mothers to frighten their children into obedience."

"Nonsense. Because of me you are glorified on earth." Jeshua dismissed Lazarus' comment. "Sit." He slapped the ground. "Ironic, isn't it? You exist because I made you exist and now I exist only because you exist. The glory which you gave me I have given you. We are one. I am as much a prisoner of your miracle as you are of my history."

Lazarus swallowed just enough wine to wet his throat. His face screwed up in disgust at the acrid taste.

Jeshua tossed his empty goatskin to the side. "What did you expect, a special vintage from Herod's private stock?" He snatched the wine bag from Lazarus.

"No, I expect answers."

"Answers I'm out of. Questions I've got plenty of. It's how I teach. Spin a little parable and ask my followers what they make of it."

Lazarus jabbed his finger into Jeshua's chest. "You drove my wife mad."

"No one can drive someone else mad. It is faith alone that makes us lunatics and fanatics."

"Cure her. Give her back to me."

Jeshua finished the contents of the second goatskin. "No more miracles. No more questions. No more wine," he solemnly intoned as he tried to get to his feet but sank to the earth.

Lazarus locked his hands around the drunken Messiah's forearm and pulled him to his feet. "If you have the power, you must help me."

"Lord, though I am ready to go with you, both unto prison and to death, I cannot help you. The power and the glory are not mine." Jeshua hugged Lazarus' neck. "Walk with me."

Lazarus turned his face away from the rank breath of Jeshua. "You're filled with more spirit than religion."

Peter burst through the stand of trees with the Zebedee brothers as Lazarus and Jeshua approached the pool. "I will lead my Master!" He tried to haul Jeshua away by his arm. It was a futile effort. Peter's muscles were no match for those of a man who had spent his childhood toting logs for his father and his youth pitching drunken guests out of his mother's inn.

"From this day on, no one is allowed to touch me," Jeshua snarled. "Tell all the lepers, the crippled, the blind to find someone else's robe to hold onto. I want peace while there is still time allotted to me on earth."

Peter brandished a sword. "Master, men are coming to arrest you. If you don't leave with me now, you won't have a lot of time to ponder your future."

"Then let them come to take this cup from my lips!" Jeshua raised his wine sack. He wrung the last few red beads from it.

A noisy mob comprised of Sadducees and Pharisees alike crashed through the grove. Peter's sword flashed in the moonlight. He sought out a path of escape. It was no use. Herod's palace guards and Roman soldiers blocked off every potential avenue of flight.

Jeshua laid his hand on Peter's shoulder. "Put away your weapon. Am I not obliged to drink from the cup which my father has given me?"

"Not if I can help it," Lazarus shouted. He tackled Jeshua, rolling into a ravine concealed by the grove's wild undergrowth. Peter followed them into the gully. The Zebedee brothers came to Peter's aid and fell on top of the three of them. The struggle was over as quickly as it had begun.

A figure with a camel hair sleeve torn from his coat staggered out of the brambles. The Zebedee brothers and Peter appeared behind him, supporting a limp and bruised body between them.

From out of the crowd a man wearing a brown hooded robe stepped forward. He pushed back the mantle's cowl, exposing the face of the priest who had guided Lazarus and James to Matthew's house. "Is this him?" he asked, looking over his shoulder.

Judas threaded his way through the mob. He walked past the brothers, casting a quick glance at them, and reached out to touch the chestnut-coloured coat of the one he had chosen to betray.

"Is this him?" Caiaphas asked again.

Judas closed his eyes. "He is the one I choose."

Barely had the words escaped Judas' lips when Caiaphas commanded, "Seize him."

The chosen one lifted his head, staring at Judas through one eye. He started to speak but was silenced by an elbow slamming into his mouth. The crowd closed in on him and kicked his legs out from underneath him. They pinned his arms behind his back and dropped a burlap sack over his head. Fists, feet, clubs, anything that that could inflict injury, pummelled him. Soon the burlap bag was soaked with blood. In the confusion Peter and the brothers managed to flee through the grove, dragging their spiritless captive with them.

From the centre of the rabble a rope was passed along. Only the presence of the Romans prevented the mob's frenzy from escalating into a lynching. A soldier intercepted the length of hemp by using his helmeted head to butt senseless the last man to touch it. He shoved the rope into Judas' hands. Caiaphas snapped his fingers. The guards lifted the semi-conscious body of their prisoner by his arms and legs and carried him out of Gethsemane.

"He's ours after you get finished with him," a centurion barked.

"Why? He's not accused of a capital crime," Caiaphas responded. "He is being questioned about his beliefs. If they prove false he will be sent to where he can be helped to see the error of his ways."

"If he is the one that some people claim is the King of the Jews, he has committed a capital crime in Rome's eyes. There is no king but Caesar."

"He's a gadfly, but I believe he's harmless," Caiaphas said. "With the judicious application of reason he will gladly retire to his colony of Essenes and trouble neither of us any longer."

The centurion trapped a firefly that was circling his head. "If he's tried for sedition, guilty or not, I warrant that he'll bother no one anymore." The soldier pounded his leather breast in salute to the high priest and marched after the crowd.

Caiaphas returned the Roman's courtesy, lightly tapping his chest with his fingertips. When the mob passed out of sight, Caiaphas dipped into his purse. He tossed a bag of coins on the ground. "Thirty pieces of silver, how far do you think that will take us?"

Judas stooped over to retrieve the bag of coins. "With luck it may provide our men with a few more swords and spears."

"Betrayed by a kiss," Caiaphas muttered.

"He was betrayed by his own lack of purpose." Judas jingled the silver inside the pouch. "It will be remembered as the embrace that saved a nation." He stuffed the bag under the belt of his robe and walked to the other side of the grove.

Judas waited for over an hour under a leafless olive tree. The mob's jeers and shouts of victory drifted through the garden as it marched toward Jerusalem. The tree had ceased to bear fruit long before the Romans humiliated Israel. A Samaritan legend identified it as the tree where Absalom was slain while dangling by his hair from its branches. Although David had cursed the tree, it had survived past his kingdom as a symbol of the great king's failure to please God.

Peter emerged from his hiding place, a tool shed a hundred yards away from Judas' tree. Behind him stood the Zebedee brothers. "It is done?"

"It is done," Judas responded.

"Good."

Like a half-filled sack of grain, their hostage, abducted from under the Romans' noses, lay on the ground covered with a blanket. "What about him?" Judas asked.

"We'll bring him to Qumran. They will know what to do with him there." Peter removed the rope coiled around Judas' shoulder. "Who knows? Perhaps he will even thank us one day for removing the burden of his calling from him."

Judas nervously fingered the pouch of silver tucked under his belt. "It's going to be hard to keep this a secret. The truth is bound to come to out with so many involved."

Peter waited for Judas to turn his back on him. "It will only get out if someone lets it out." He bashed Judas on the head with a carpenter's mallet.

173

The concussion of the blow did not kill Judas. He was stunned, but still aware of the prickly fibres of the rope biting into his neck. Peter tossed the end of the rope over the stoutest limb of the bare tree.

"Get over here. I can't do it by myself."

The brothers hesitated before lending Peter a hand. Together the three disciples hauled on the rope. Judas' feet dangled inches away from solid earth.

Peter waited for the body to cease its spasms. He bowed his head and recited the Shema. Judas swayed in the wind. The coins in his purse clinked together like small chimes.

"Forgive them, for they know not what they do," groaned the blanketed lump on the ground, reeking of sour wine.

"Take him to Qumran," Peter commanded the brothers.

"What if someone wants to know who he is?" asked Raham, the younger of the brothers.

"After tonight it's doubtful if anyone will remember or care who he is or was." Peter reflected. "If the question arises, do as I will do. Deny that you know him."

# 23

Throughout the night Peter loitered around the entrance of Caiaphas' mansion, where the Sanhedrin had convened to interrogate the prisoner. He warmed his hands over a fire burning in a kiln in the courtyard. A serving maid accompanied by a novice Levite walked out of the house carrying a basin of brown water. She paused in front of Peter.

"I was at the gates of the city when he entered Jerusalem last Sunday. Strange how many who loved him then now hate him." She squinted at Peter. "Weren't you with him when he arrived?"

Peter moved out of the light of the fire. "Woman, I have never known him or met him."

"Say that again." The Levite, who had come with the maid to prevent her from dashing off to spread the news about the Sanhedrin's trial, quizzed Peter. "He is said to be a Galilean and you have the accent from that part of the country."

"Man, I am not from there. In my travels I've picked up a touch of every region's manner of speaking."

"That's too bad. The poor fellow needs a friend right now." The Levite waited for the maid to dump the tainted liquid in the basin and refill it with fresh water. "They've cursed him, spat on him and whipped him for over three hours trying to get him to admit to his heresy."

"How many times do I have to tell you? I don't know this man. He is of no concern to me."

A cock crowed as the Levite hurried the maid through the door, slamming it behind him. Peter pressed his ear to the door. He heard the angry voices of the inquisitors berating their captive. He searched the courtyard until he discovered an empty olive oil amphora. He rolled the clay jug to the door on its base and flipped it over. He stood on it, peeking through the openings of the lintel. A guard tied a blindfold around the prisoner's eyes.

Annas, Caiaphas' son-in-law, tiptoed up to the prisoner. "Prophet, I hear that you know everything that was, is, or will be," he said, and punched him in the face. "So tell me who is it who struck you?"

"Leave him alone." An emaciated man dressed in a green satin robe and wearing a three-cornered hat hobbled into the middle of the foyer. The man's gout-inflamed feet were wrapped in cotton gauze soaked in essence of cloves. He was surrounded by masked bodyguards. He rapped the silver knob of his walking staff on the marble floor. One of the guards prevented Annas from striking the prisoner again.

"We are here to determine whether this fellow is guilty of blasphemy or treason. We are not here to amuse ourselves by torturing him." The man's voice was as thin and reedy as his consumptive body. "Is that not correct, Caiaphas?" He glanced up at the high priest who sat with the other judges on a gallery overlooking the chamber.

"As you say, my Lord Herod," Caiaphas answered, thinking at the same time that it was prudent that Herod's bodyguards wore masks. If their identities were known they would not survive long on the streets outside the palace walls.

Herod lifted his staff and tapped the heretic on his shoulder. "Are you the Christ? Tell us."

A bloodied, mangled face raised its chin in defiance. "If I tell you, you will not believe me. And if also I ask you the same, you will not answer me, nor let me go."

"Don't play with me." Herod rolled the staff lightly across the prisoner's shoulder. "I am a patient man, indulgent to an extent beyond most men. I tolerated the lies and slanders of your cousin many years before I acted. But my patience is finite. Answer me this: Are you Jeshua, the one who says he is the Son of God?"

A look of unbridled hatred was directed at Herod through the man's one real eye. "You say that I am."

"Seize him and take him to Pilate," Herod squealed.

Caiaphas rose from his seat to address the other members of the Sanhedrin. "Do we need any further witness? For we ourselves have heard his insolence from his own mouth." He ran down from the gallery to the chamber. "He must be banished from the city and sent into the desert to repent of his blasphemy. Until this occurs he is to be considered dead by our people." Caiaphas inserted himself between Herod's guards and the prisoner. "I have given my judgement. He is dead."

Challenged by a mere priest, Herod smiled benignly. In a gentle voice that concealed the rage growing inside him, he said, "Symbolically, perhaps. Unfortunately, Caesar does not put a lot of stock in symbols. You have found him guilty in a religious court, but he still has to answer to Rome for his crimes."

"Since when can a foreign court hold a man culpable for exercising, however wrong-minded, his pursuit of a living Torah?"

"Enough of this! Our nation is teetering on the brink of insurrection because of a proliferation of prophets and would-be Messiahs. My words alone should be sufficient for you to heed. But, seeing as how you place credence in no one but your own, read this letter from Lord Gamaliel commanding you to turn this man over to the Romans." Herod slapped a parchment scroll into Caiaphas' hands. The priest read it slowly then gave it back to Herod. He nodded at the novice Levite. The young Levite forced the burlap sack, encrusted with dried blood, over the heretic's head.

"You priests come with me," Herod ordered. "Pilate does not want this one's blood on Rome's hands alone. If he is to die, it will be because of crimes committed against Israel's God and Rome's authority."

The guards herded the judges of the Sanhedrin down the gallery's stairs. As the cortege of priests and guards left Caiaphas' mansion, it was greeted by a mob of more than a hundred men who demanded that Jeshua be released to them. Peter hid at the rear of the crowd. He avoided looking at the prisoner as Herod's procession passed by him.

When the crowd arrived at the fortress of Antonio, they found Pilate waiting for them at the top of the stairs. He was wearing a plain white tunic with a red shoulder sash that designated him as an official of Rome. Behind him, frozen at attention, were fifty heavily-armed centurions wearing full battle dress. Pilate lifted an ivory sceptre capped by a war eagle. In unison the troops extended their shields in front of them. They marched down the stairs and onto the plaza, shoving the people back from the landing. The mob split in two when Herod's guards propelled the heretic through their midst.

Pilate leisurely descended the stairs and strolled around the prisoner. "And of what is he accused?" he asked. It was a legal formality, for in Rome, even the lowest citizen had the right to hear the crimes of which he was charged.

"As promised, we have delivered to you a preacher of insurrection. We have found him perverting the nation and forbidding the people to give tribute to Caesar, saying that he himself is Christ, a king," Herod answered.

A wave of laughter rolled through the crowd when Pilate patted Herod on his head like a faithful lap dog. The Roman governor lifted the bottom of the sack covering the accused rebel's head. The man winced but refused to scream when Pilate clamped his hand on his broken jaw.

"Are you the King of the Jews?"

"You say I am."

"His answer is hardly worthy of death." Pilate turned to the commander of the soldiers. "See if you can loosen this halfwit's tongue." Lysias detached a whip from his girdle and tossed it to one of his men.

The soldiers hauled the prisoner up the stairs and into the fortress. The sound of the lash being applied with enough ferocity to kill a normal person could be heard in the plaza. When they returned with the scourged man, a purple robe was draped over his back.

Lysias removed the sack from the prisoner's head. The damaged face that greeted him was one that he had held in his dreams since Revivim. "Every king needs a crown," he said.

A soldier ran into the fort and fetched a metal loop with spikes attached inside the band. Lysias pushed the loop around the prisoner's forehead and tightened a screw. As the circumference of the band constricted, the spikes pierced flesh. A torrent of fresh blood flowed down the prisoner's face.

"Now you are a king," Pilate declared. "But are you the King of the Jews?"

"My kingdom is not of this earth."

Pilate sucked in his breath at the man's enigmatic reply. "Oh, do shut up. The only part of paradise you are assured of having is the dirt to cover your disgusting corpse." Pilate faced Herod. "We have three executions scheduled for this day and four potential candidates for the honour. Seeing as how this is some sort of holy day for you people, I will give you a choice of who should be crucified." Pilate glanced at Lysias once more. "Have the other one brought out." Within minutes a filthy one-eyed man secured in a neck collar, iron shackles and manacles was beaten and kicked from the fort.

"I don't really care who dies," Pilate said. "My only concern is that I have an empty cross on Calvary, and I have to fill it."

"It is your decision," Herod responded.

"Nonsense, old friend. As far as I can ascertain, the only crime this idiot you presented is guilty of is stubbornness." Pilate dipped his hands into a basin of water that was placed before him. He washed the blood of the prisoner from his soft skin. "Now, this one," Pilate said, poking the one-eyed man in the stomach, "should be of special interest to you. He led the attack on your wife's and step-daughter's caravan.

Only your god knows what would have happened to them if the trap we had set had failed."

Herod shook with fury. "Set the mystic free and make Barabbas die in agony," he was about to scream, when a chant exploded from the crowd.

"Release unto us Barabbas." Gamaliel had carefully selected and prompted his plants in the mob. "Away with this man and crucify the blasphemer, the preacher of sedition."

Pilate looked at Herod with an expression of detached amusement. He knew that if the puppet king were to maintain his tenuous grip on power he had to follow the wishes of the rabble, no matter what his personal feelings were.

"Free the bandit," Herod muttered.

"Excuse me? I didn't hear you," Pilate needled Herod.

"Release the robber."

"Agreed."

The soldiers unshackled Barabbas. The bandit limped past the man who would take his place on the hill of execution, Golgotha, a place littered with the skulls and bones of just men and criminals alike. He paused when the condemned man choked out a plea for him to stop. The prisoner lifted his hands to his face and dug his thumb into his eye socket.

"Here, you need it more than I do," he said and placed an almond-shaped stone with an eyeball painted on its surface in Barabbas' palm. Barabbas feigned a smile and winked with his good eye before a soldier kneed him in the back, sending him tumbling down the stairs.

"Let it be known that I am innocent of the blood of this person: see you to it." Again Pilate washed his hands and held them up for the crowd to see. He invoked a prayer to his gods to appease the spirit of the condemned man so it would look elsewhere for revenge.

# 24

Since Flavius' miraculous escape from the ambush set by the Zealots, and his subsequent assignment to the garrison in Jerusalem, he had cultivated an abiding hatred of everything within Israel. His antipathy for the Jews intensified when he heard that the bandit who had slaughtered and mutilated his comrades had been set free by Pilate and Herod. Despite his protest to Lysias, the only man who detested the land and its people as much as he did, Flavius was assigned to oversee the crucifixion. To ensure the mystic was made to suffer, he ordered the centurions to drive nails through the man's wrists and feet as a message to others that no one, not even so-called Messiahs, can escape the wrath of Caesar.

He saw no reason to supervise the preliminary details of the execution. He sent word up the hill to his men to advise him when the condemned man was ready to give up the ghost. He wanted to be on hand to record the hour of the prisoner's demise.

After eight hours had passed, Flavius was disappointed to hear from a soldier who came to the fort that the mystic appeared ready to expire. Flavius had seen enough crucifixions in his youth along the roads in his homeland to know that the shortest execution lasted an average of twenty hours. He took his spear from its corner in the barracks and followed the soldier. The sky grew darker the nearer he came to Golgotha. He held a laurel leaf under his nose as he started up the hill to lessen the stench of the open-pit grave at the crest of the hill.

As Flavius approached the top of Golgotha, he caught a glimpse of a black-haired woman dressed in a saffron-coloured kaftan. He was certain he had seen her somewhere in the past. She reached up to touch the feet of the man occupying the centre crucifix, then vanished into the crowd which had assembled to taunt the three men suspended on the T-shaped crosses.

Flavius ordered the spectators to disperse, warning them that crucifixes were the one commodity of which there was no shortage in Jerusalem. He looked up at the broken body of the man suspended on the middle cross. A sign attached to the top of the crucifix, "The King of the Jews," brought a smile to his face.

Flavius flipped his spear over, placed its butt under the man's chin, and lifted his head so that he could make out his features in the fading daylight. He jumped back when the man vomited a stomach full of blood. The man stared at him through one eye.

*"Eloi, Lama Sabachthani?"* he cried out, and slumped lifelessly on the cross.

One of the soldiers poked Flavius with his elbow. "Didn't last long, did he? Truly this was the son of God," he mocked.

Flavius waited for an hour at the base of the cross, the prescribed amount of time to validate that all life had been extinguished. He flipped his spear over and circled the cross, checking for signs of life. He touched the cold toes of the crucified man and tickled the bottoms of his feet. The body remained motionless.

The soldier who had laughed held an iron bar. He aimed it at the dead man's legs but halted in mid-swing when Flavius ordered him to get away. Flavius whirled around and pierced the corpse's rib cage with the head of his spear. A copious amount of blood mixed with water spurted from his side. "If he's not dead yet, nothing will kill him," he said to himself.

Flavius picked up a sponge floating in bucket of water, wrung it out and wiped his face. The sponge had been soaked in vinegar and burnt his eyes.

The soldier waited until Flavius had stopped grimacing and said, "There are some people here who want to take the body away with them."

"Give him to them and report back to me where they've taken him."

For two nights Flavius concealed himself behind an outcrop of rocks in the burial hills of Jerusalem. On the sunrise of the third day three men, each carrying a thick pole and a bag, climbed up to the mouth of a cave sealed by a boulder. At first they tried to move the boulder by throwing their shoulders against it. Their struggle was to no avail. The rock would not budge. Finally two of the men planted the ends of their poles under the rock and used them as levers to roll the stone away. From inside the cave a howl of outrage chilled the air. The terrified men dropped their poles and chased one another down the hill.

The tomb's occupant stumbled into the morning light. He tore the winding sheet from his body and squatted in front of the bags the men had left on the ground. In the first bag was a jug of water, a pot of cheese and a loaf of bread. He tore off a piece of bread and held it between his teeth as he rummaged through the other bags. In the second sack was a change of garments, a white robe, a chestnut-coloured coat missing a sleeve, and a pair of sandals. In the last bag he found a knife, a short club, and a leather helmet. He looked at the hills above him when Flavius shifted his weight and started a miniature avalanche of pebbles. He stared with his one eye for what seemed an eternity, then slipped the knife through the belt of his robe and placed the helmet over his head. He tramped down the hill, swinging the club up and down, smashing an invisible opponent's skull.

Flavius left his hiding place and walked toward the cave, stopping to pick up the winding sheet. He carried it into the tomb, placing it on the stone table where the condemned man had been laid to rest. He remained inside the cave, pondering whether his debt was now truly cleared.

Women's voices could be heard outside the cave. The woman Flavius had recognised the day of the crucifixion on Golgotha stood at the entrance of the tomb. "Stay where you are," he commanded. "I know whom you seek and he is no longer here, for he has risen."

# 25

More than three decades had passed since the man cast off his name. Since that time those who spoke of him, when they dared to mention him at all, called him Adlai, Justice of the Lord. It was whispered that he sought solace among the rotting cadavers of Israel when he was not slaying its enemies.

Despite wearing a black-and-white hooded Levite's cloak and a leather jersey and breeches, Adlai was impervious to the heat. He had waited for hours by the side of the road leading to Damascus. Word had arrived that the leader of a new sect of Jews was on his way to Corinth to join up with his followers. From Damascus the apostle of this movement would board a boat and sail to Greece, and from there journey to Rome to preach to the gentiles.

Adlai was patient. He knew the leader of the infant religious sect would travel this way. He sat cross-legged with a long club embedded with barbed spikes across his lap. He was beyond letting the small nuisances of life perturb him. Flies hovering around his head landed occasionally on his face and wandered undisturbed in and out of the hole of his empty eye socket.

The road to Damascus had been worn smooth by thousands of Roman soldiers who had marched along it during the great revolt. Adlai's fleshless smile stretched across his teeth. It was a blessing that Gamaliel had not lived to see the outcome of his cherished uprising. Jerusalem no longer existed. The Temple was razed, a feed pen built on its site to house swine.

A donkey bearing an ancient man riding sidesaddle meandered down the road. The old man cooled himself with a fan made of orange rice paper. Adlai stepped into the middle of the road, blocking the rider's path.

The old man lisped, "Get out of the way."

Adlai tossed back the hood of his robe. "Is that any way to speak to a friend?"

"Twice on my way to Damascus I've encountered the crimes of my youth," the old man wailed. "Forgive me. I'm a changed man, believe me."

"I'm not here to give you absolution." Adlai rested his weight on the end of his club as if it were a walking stick.

"Well, if you're going to detain me you might as well help me down." The old man held out his arms. "The years have been good to you," he remarked wistfully as he looked into Adlai's face. "Considering what you had to start with."

Adlai scooped the old man out of the saddle. "Thirty, forty, even a hundred years are nothing in the life of a man sentenced to immortality, Saul."

"Paul. Since my epiphany, I call myself Paul." The old man surveyed his surroundings. He remembered aloud that it was on this same road that he had encountered Jeshua after his brief escape from Qumran. "He wasn't free long. One of his disciples saw him and informed the Essenes. They tracked him down and returned him to his cave. But you already know that, Lazarus."

Adlai winced when he heard the name he had buried on a scrap of parchment with Rachel. She had chosen to serve out her life tending to the needs of her Master in his cell in Qumran. With her passing, Lazarus had ceased to exist.

"I visited Jeshua before he died." Adlai set Paul down. "I don't know what tortured him more during his last years at Qumran — his followers abandoning him that night, or your taking up his cause."

Paul whisked away the flies with his fan. "He never had a cause."

Adlai nodded in agreement. "Everyone used him."

Paul daintily pressed his fingertips to the pink lips protruding from his white beard. "That's what Messiahs are for." He could not help but be amused by the memory that his old adversary, Gamaliel, had intended to use Jeshua as martyr to stir the nation into a suicidal insurrection against Rome. "Now look — Gamaliel, James, even that scoundrel Barabbas are dead and it is left up to me to spread the Gospel," he reminisced.

Adlai raked his fingers through his tangled beard. "The version of the tale you spread has zero to do with the man I knew or the story that I lived."

Paul doodled in the dirt, tracing the outline of a fish with the handle of his fan. "I changed the focus of the story, but kept the hero. I just altered him to fit a stronger nation's vision of the truth."

"There is only one truth, the one that I lived," Adlai said.

Paul flicked his fan as though that action was sufficient to disarm Adlai. "My version of the story is one that gentiles will come to accept."

What Paul said was true. He had created a god very much like Rome's gods: a god born of a virgin, a woman impregnated by a god. The myth would be transformed as needed to correspond to the pagans' beliefs until eventually it would be impossible to see where Hashem began and Zeus ended.

"This is crap!" Adlai gritted his teeth. "To think I bore the pain of his trial for you. Can you honestly tell me that you love those who have ground us under their boots and have turned us against one another?"

"I don't love Rome. I love the Pax Romana." Paul's ancient body trembled as he forced himself to his feet. "Before Caesar, we slaughtered one another over such articles of faith as what shade of red the sacrificial bullock is."

Adlai placed his club behind his neck like a yoke. "I was sent to hear you out and decide whether you should be allowed to live." He held the ends of the club, twisting from side to side as he spoke.

"Your decision?"

Adlai raised the club above his head. "You shouldn't."

"So you'll murder me." Paul tucked his chin into the top of his robe and thrust his neck out. "Aim here. If it doesn't kill me, at least I won't experience any pain while waiting for the second blow."

Adlai shoved his club into a cowhide tube worn over his back. "It will be interesting to see what kind of reception you get in Rome." He walked to the donkey and picked up its tether. "For the cause," he said as he left the path and headed into the desert.

"Wait, Lazarus, wait," Paul called out. "Come with me. Stand as the visible truth of the power of —" Paul cringed when Adlai whirled around.

"What do you know of power? All power is given unto me in heaven and earth!" The wind rose up to lash the desert, burying history under the sands. Adlai trudged toward Masada carrying the secret of his nation with him and asked, "What do you know of truth?"

# Epilogue

Schubert's *Unfinished Symphony* was playing over the loudspeakers when the Americans liberated the camp. The S.S. guards had fled less than an hour before the allies' arrival. Prisoners huddled together like straw men throughout the compound, their huge heads wobbling on necks attached to skeletal frames.

Corporal Shapiro plodded through the officers' section of the compound. He stepped off the cobblestone path to look at the rows of flowers and shrubbery in a meticulously landscaped garden. He crushed the obscenely nourished vegetation into the rich black earth, then stepped out of the flower bed and back on to the cobblestone path. He proceeded to scrape off the clumps of mud that clung to the soles of his boots on the base of a bronze statue of a young man. The statue was naked to the waist. With one arm it held a rifle above its head; the other arm extended in a salute to the author of its nation's atrocities.

The corporal unslung his Thompson from his shoulder. He aimed it at the statue. "Never again," he promised, turning away from the monument. The barrel of his machine gun pointed at a large brick building adorned by three chimneys. "Couldn't see it happening, huh? Bullshit! You can see the smoke twenty-three miles away."

The iron door leading into the building was padlocked. The corporal sprayed the hinge with a short burst from his tommy-gun. He broke the door free of its mountings with one kick. The sudden escape of methane gas, mixed with the putrid odour of spoiled meat, forced him to his knees. It was his fourth camp. He should have been used to the stench by now. He wasn't. He doubled over, vomiting the contents of his stomach outside the threshold of the building. He wiped the mucous dribbling out of his nose on his sleeve and entered the building. His stomach crawled to the middle of his throat. He clutched his gut, retching violently, praying that there was something left in him to toss up.

"Hey, soldier, are you okay?" his sergeant asked from outside the building.

Shapiro's throat burned. "Get in here, sarge."

"Holy Jesus!" The sergeant took several deep breaths. "Okay, soldier, let's get hold of ourselves."

They slowly walked past the rows of cast-iron doors running the length of the wall facing them. Some of the doors were open just wide enough to give them glimpses of the interior of the ovens, still containing the smouldering ashes of the last victims shoved into the fire on rolling baking trays like lumps of grey bread dough.

"Bastards," Shapiro swore.

They forced their eyes to return to the original object of their horror. In one corner of the crematorium were the naked, virtually fleshless bodies of people of uncertain gender piled in stacks up to eight feet high like cords of firewood. A hollow, distant moan coming from the stack of corpses filled the emptiness of the chamber.

The sergeant slashed his hand across his throat, signalling for silence. He approached the grotesque heap of rotting corpses, all the time holding his breath to avoid inhaling the stench. A shriek came from the centre of the mound of cadavers. The screech pierced the base of his spine like an ice pick, leaving him paralyzed.

"Sarge, look out!" Shapiro's frantic warning brought him back to his senses. The sergeant hit the deck and rolled across the floor. An avalanche of stinking corpses collapsed on top of him. He struggled to his feet, kicking and flailing at the the faces of the dead, staring opened-mouthed at him as though trying to suck the life force from him. He attempted to retreat from the bodies but stopped when he felt a tug at the bottom of his fatigues. He looked down and struggled to control his urge to flee. A bony hand clawed at the fabric of his pants. A hideous face, scarred with ravages going beyond starvation and torture, rose from the floor and peered with one eye at the sergeant. The sound of the survivor's laboured breathing was deafening.

"Sarge, he's alive. Thank God, he's really fucking alive."

When the medics arrived, Shapiro and the sergeant were sitting on the ground outside the crematorium. The head of the survivor was resting in the corporal's lap.

The medics gave the survivor a small mouthful of water and a soda biscuit. They knew that the shock of a sudden intake of food would finish the job the Germans had started. Amazingly, the survivor tried to push himself to a sitting position. He stroked the corporal's cheek.

"Take it easy, mister," the chief medic said. "Ya'll are really one lucky guy."

The survivor stretched his colourless lips across his gums in a sardonic smile. His body rattled as if he were laughing at a joke that only he could understand. "Yes, lucky," he replied in an accent the soldier had never heard on the streets of Savannah. "So lucky," he repeated and began to chant.

"What's he doing?" the chief medic asked, as his two partners loaded the emaciated body of the survivor onto a stretcher.

Shapiro stood up. "He's saying Kaddish."

"I heard some fellows singing it at the other camps."

"There are not enough of us left to pray for all the dead." Shapiro slung his Thompson over his shoulder and walked off reciting the Shema as they carried away the stretcher.

"Well, can you beat that?" the medic asked and lit a Camel.

The sergeant uncoiled himself from the ground. He plucked the smoke from the medic's lips and took a hit. "Not in two thousand years," he said and handed the medic back his cigarette.